Time Travels of an Irish Psychic

Sheila Lindsay

Ariel Books
Dublin

Copyright © Sheila Lindsay 1989, 1995

First published by The Mercier Press, Cork, in 1989
ISBN 0-85342-896-4

The right of Sheila Lindsay to be identified as the author of this work has been asserted by her in accordance with the Copyright, Designs and Patents Act 1988.

All rights to this new edition, and the earlier edition, are reserved. No part of this publication may be reproduced, stored in a retrieval system, or transmitted, in any form or by any other means, electronic, facsimile, recording or otherwise without the prior written permission of the publisher.

Ariel Books is an imprint of Parkgate Publications

Parkgate Publications Ltd
19 Montague Street
Dublin 2   Ireland

Tel: 01 475 8778

ISBN 0-9523109-3-7

Printed by Mount Salus Press, Dublin

Contents

Foreword — 4

Part I: Time Travels

Chapter I	First Encounters	7
Chapter II	Psychic Awareness	10
Chapter III	The Ancient Wisdom	16
Chapter IV	Light on *The Book of Kells*	31
Chapter V	A Special Place	36

Part II: Our Links with the Cosmos

Chapter VI	Cosmic Awareness	40
Chapter VII	New Age Psychology	51
Chapter VIII	Time and Light	62
Chapter IX	Metaphysical Values	71
Chapter X	Reincarnation	80
Chapter XI	Meditation	81
Chapter XII	Sunrise	86

Foreword

THE WORLD is changing rapidly, people are so aware of possibilities, their minds are opening to a shift in consciousness, to a world of Love and Light and Peace and Joy.

There is now a great interest in our ancient sites which are built on the natural earth energies that denote, in certain places where they cross, the spiritual energies available to renew the whole self.

Bus loads of people come and are rushed in and out of our ancient stones, being told by official guides that these are all burial sites.

This is no more logical than saying that the great cathedrals are burial sites. Bodies may have been interred there many years later, but that was not the original purpose for the raising of the stones.

In this re-issue of my book, more and more people will find the Truth, as they did when it was first published. Then they telephoned me, wrote to me and wanted me to come and talk.

It woke something deep down in their consciousness - a folk memory that was deeply ingrained, going back many generations, many incarnations.

People want to visit these places alone, to sit and meditate and absorb whatever knowledge each will give them.

It was through Helen O'Clery that I first found my gift of being able to travel back in time. This gave me information that was later proved to be correct. Thank you, Helen. My thanks also go to Carole Devaney who edited the book and pulled it into shape.

SHEILA LINDSAY,
May 1995

Part I

Time Travels

First Encounters

It was a warm day, the sun shining down on the circle of granite stones set in the field below us. We were walking down a slope of bright green grass, leaving the woods behind. Below was a stream and beyond that the stone circle.

Coming up from the circle was a great sheet of white light. The stones alone were making the light. We waited and watched for some time. Then from one of the larger stones, a bright pink light shot up, which after a while changed to yellow. Then some blue light appeared low down on the left. It was a spectacular sight, all that circle of white light with streaks of pink and yellow and blue shooting through it.

A person dressed in a flowing brown robe appeared beside us; he looked at us in a friendly way. For some reason I expected him to be dressed in white; I asked him why he was in brown and what was happening. He tried to explain, but though I knew he was talking I was not able to hear what he said.

Down at the circle, a white-robed figure was walking around the stones. The light had now settled down to just a glow at each stone; the person seemed to be checking each one, almost like an engineer checking his power station.

Presently, more 'white people' came — a river of white-robed figures flowing towards the circle. I got the impression that they were expecting something. Then I saw yellow light coming up in the distance. The figure at the circle held out his arms in salutation to the light.

Suddenly, a black menacing shape appeared in the sky, flying rapidly towards the circle. It was long and narrow, with black things like twisted spokes trailing from it. The person at the circle saw the thing approaching and was obviously horrified. He turned light at it from one of the stones, trying to stop it. But he was not strong enough alone — he needed more white people. They came hurrying, and shot light up from the stones at the black object, like a search light beamed on it. They stopped its advance and followed it with the light as it sped away.

When the object had gone from sight, the people drew the light back until it settled gently again at each stone. They all appeared to be happy and full of joy at having protected their circle.

The pictures that had been so vivid suddenly faded. I came back to the present, to the circle as it is now, with some of its stones standing, some fallen and others possibly missing.

I was at the Piper's Stones in Athgreany, Co Wicklow, beyond Blessington on the road to Carlow. From the site, there is a wide view over the countryside, with hills rising behind the circle; away in the distance was what appeared to be a mound with the top caved in.

I had come to the Piper's Stones with Helen O'Clery, who was to record the experiment. This was the first of our archaeological investigations. We always followed the same pattern: I talked about what I saw and Helen wrote the notes. At first I walked around the circle, touching each stone in turn, feeling the life in it, loving it, getting to know it, and yet very much aware that at some time in another life, I had known these stones well and was now renewing an ancient friendship. Having touched them all, I felt that there was one special stone that would talk to me. I sat with my back against it, Helen beside me with her notebook. I asked to be shown what the circle was for, prayed for protection and went into deep meditation. I travelled back in time and the pictures came — more vivid in my mind than the present.

From what I had witnessed, this stone circle seemed to be a light centre that had been used to protect the country from attack. In some way, the 'white people' I had seen were able to generate powerful light beams. Or did they bring light down from the sun and store it until it was needed? Were these stones generators of energy, or were they storage batteries? I did not know the answers. But I was encouraged to have got such clear pictures. I felt excited and happy, but tired, as if I had made a long journey. I always did feel tired after each of these expeditions into the past.

At every ancient site we visited, I was going back to previous lives, in which obviously I had worked with the stones. There was always a brown-robed friend there when I went back. The more I saw of the great stones, the more convinced I became that they must be brought back to life and used as they were meant to be used. They were each tuned in to cosmic influences. They were like a musical instrument, an organ, waiting to be played. People had forgotten how to use them. When the ice came and covered the land, the people who understood the stones left. When the ice melted, other people came but they did not know about the stones; they did not know what they were for or how to use them. They turned some of the ancient sites into burial places and used others for their own ceremonial purposes.

It is only within the last two hundred years that a few people here and there have had the vision to realise the purpose for which these sites were built. They were scorned and laughed at by 'flat-earth' archaeologists who had no knowledge of astronomy. But an archaeologist without astronomy is groping in the dark.

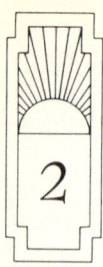

Psychic Awareness

Time — past, present and future — is all around us like a great ocean. I can never think of time as a straight line, where we move from past to present to future to finality. This seems to me to be quite illogical. The ocean of time is all around us; as with the ocean at the seaside, some of us are better swimmers than others. People who have the gift of perception can move easily through time. They can move forwards or backwards or parallel, so that they can see the future or the past, and they can also see the present as a parallel experience in another place.

People with this gift were known in the olden days as prophets, foretellers or soothsayers. Today, they are usually known as psychics. Life can be extremely difficult for such people, especially as children born into a materialistic family. They are so aware of things that other people are totally unaware of; they know and see what other people do not know and see. They are made to feel 'queer', to feel different, to be treated as if they were almost insane. They are told to stop imagining things, to stop telling lies. And so they gradually withdraw, go into themselves and do not talk any more about what they know and see. Their own world is so much lovelier and kinder than this material world they do not understand.

I am firmly convinced that many people who are certified as mentally ill are, in fact, psychic people whose gifts have been suppressed. If they had had the opportunity to meet other people like themselves who understood them, their psychic gifts would have developed and been used as they were intended to be used.

As a psychic myself, I had a difficult childhood and early life through lack of understanding from those around me. This caused me great self-doubt and a feeling of inferiority, of being different. I was fortunate, however, in later life when I met people like myself. It was such relief to be able to talk openly, to feel completely at ease, to discover that there were many people like me. I was not the odd one out any more; my gifts began to develop, as I could now use them openly.

I had so often seen the future and been afraid to tell people of what I knew would happen. There was no point in warning them in advance about coming problems, nor in telling them about the time to come when a present problem would be over and good things would happen. They would have ignored what I said or laughed at it. But now, at last, I was with friends on my own wavelength. They soon discovered that if I put my hands in a pair of shoes that had been recently worn, I was able to get a lot of useful information about the person who had worn them. Sometimes it was a friend or a relation of the person concerned who brought shoes belonging to someone they were worried about. Perhaps it was someone who had gone abroad and had not written, or it could be someone at home who was going through a bad time.

The information came in very clear pictures and was always relevant. Sitting in my own special armchair in my home, I would put my hands in the shoes — left hand in the left shoe, right hand in the right shoe — then go into a semi-dream state. I was not fully awake, nor was I fully asleep, but floating in a twilight zone between the two. Then in a little while I would see pictures, something between a dream and reality. They were far more real than a dream, more factual. As I saw the pictures, I talked about what I was seeing.

Distance made no difference: whether the owner of the shoes was on the far side of the world or in the same town, the pictures came in just the same way. There was one occasion when someone left her son's shoes with me and said she would come back later. He was abroad and she was worried about him. I 'read' the shoes while she was not present and wrote down what I saw. But that was unusual for me to do the writing; usually I dictated what I saw to whoever was present.

One evening, a young man came with his girlfriend's shoes. He was worried about her and did not know what was wrong. I settled down with the shoes in the usual way and talked about what I saw. After a while, I heard him speaking in a very agitated way; his words eventually penetrated and switched off the pictures. 'That light, what's that light? What's that green light around you?' He was very upset. If I had known before I started that he could see the auric light, I would have warned him that I had to switch on to a higher dimension and get my information by using the power of light.

I think that when I am functioning on this other dimension, I am using the light spectrum to bring in information. There is a great range of light, from the longest light waves to the shortest light waves, but only a small part of the spectrum is visible light. I feel that the Megalithic, or Stone Age, people understood light and used it for many things in ways that have been forgotten.

Sometimes I saw the future in dreams quite unintentionally. Sometimes as a recurring dream, perhaps four or five times, exactly the same things would be shown to me. At other times it would be one dream, so vivid and real that I knew it to be an actual event to come. The foretelling dreams were in colour; sometimes there would be one strong patch of colour of no particular shape and that colour would have a strong meaning for the person for whom the dream was intended.

When the dream was for myself, I knew that if I obeyed it implicitly things would work out exactly as I had been shown. No matter how seemingly impossible the outcome was, it did not matter; all I had to do was to obey the instructions and everything went right.

All this time I was doing little bits of writing — nothing very much, just getting a few poems and articles published. Then I met Helen at the home of mutual friends. It was a study group, interested in psychotherapeutics, that met once a week. I saw her on the far side of the room, thought she looked an interesting person and asked someone who she was. I was told, 'That's Helen O'Clery; she writes books.'

I do not remember when it was that Helen and I first discussed my gift of being able to see the future. But I do remember the first time she asked me to do it for her. She was nursing both her mother and her husband, and was very much overworked and constantly tired. She was in my house and gave me something to hold that belonged to her husband. I was aware of driving along a straight road with tall, slender trees spaced out beside it . . . driving along, driving along, then a corner. Then a crash and people were hurt. It was terrible, people were badly hurt. 'It is horrible, I must come back. I can't stay looking.'

This was an unexpected and frightening experience of what I thought was to come. But Helen said it had already happened. They had had a bad car crash in France some years ago and were seriously injured, all just as I had described it. For some reason I do not understand, I had seen the past instead of the future.

But why did I see the past this time, when before it had always been the future? She had wanted to know about the future, something to help her in the difficult time she was going through. Was the future tied up in some way with this accident in the past? I did not know the answer to that; the whole incident was bewildering.

Later on, as we got to know each other better, I discovered that she was deeply interested in archaeology, ancient history and mythology. I can only assume that I inadvertently tuned into her interest in the past, which was of many years standing and deeply ingrained. Her desire to know the future was a temporary and fleeting interest, so that I picked up the stronger of the two.

From time to time, she gave me other things to hold and see pictures with. One in particular stands out in my memory. She gave me a photograph of a small white-washed house. She told me nothing about it, not even what country it was in. On the white outside wall of the house, there were drawings in very bright colours. There were pictures of palm trees, an airplane, a boat, a train, the sun, some houses, a river, a mountain, some people, the moon and a camel. Whoever lived in the house had decorated that wall in a striking way.

I held the photograph between my palms. I seem to be able to 'see' through my hands on a different level of awareness than through my eyes. The pictures go through my hands into my brain; they are always very clear and usually represent actual happenings, although sometimes they are symbolic and need interpretation.

At first, I was aware only of some grey and some brown colour; then the picture came clearly. I was looking through narrow slits and going through arches, like a dark little street that was arched over. It was brighter to the right. Then there were lovely trees that looked like ferns. I had never seen trees like this before — a fern that was as tall as a tree was quite a new experience for me. Several times I mentioned how beautiful they were.

There were two children, one sitting, the other standing, playing with a spotted ball. A man was coming towards them; the children saw him and were obviously delighted. They seemed to know him well. He squatted down beside them, apparently telling them something very exciting. I could not hear the words spoken, but the three of them were happy. Presently they got up and walked away, the children holding the man's hands and all still talking. He seemed to be telling them a story and they were asking questions. They went past a wall with a pattern of diamond-shaped holes. There were more of the fern-like trees and houses the colour of sand. It was a hot day. They passed a bearded priest, dressed in long black clothes with a black hat, and continued along a cool avenue lined with the fern-like trees.

Then they came out into the hot sunshine, down a sloping path towards a valley. There was a high cliff on the right, all sand-coloured. After a time, I became aware of great statues carved into the cliff-face and entrances into the cliff that were not ordinary caves, but obviously cut and decorated by skilled stone-masons. It was a cliff, yet there appeared to be a building cut into its face, with these enormous statues outside.

Suddenly, I had a strange, uneasy feeling and said, 'We should not be here, everybody has gone away. We should not be here. We must go, it is not good, it is better to keep away.' Then the pictures stopped.

All the time I had been talking, Helen was writing down what I said. I asked her, 'What was all that about? It doesn't make sense to me. That had nothing at all to do with the painted house. I did not even see it.' I felt that the whole experiment had been a complete waste of time. So I was very surprised when she said, 'Yes, it did make sense. You were at Abu Simbel.'

'What's Abu Simbel? I never heard of it.'

She then told me that at Abu Simbel in Egypt, some way up the Nile, there was a very wonderful temple carved out of the cliff, by the river. Outside the temple entrance, there were four colossal statues of Ramses II and two statues of his queen, Nefertari. The whole edifice was carved out of the living rock, a magnificent work of art. A little further on was a second temple, made in the same way, with another four statues of the pharaoh.

The Egyptians decided to build a dam on the Nile for hydro-electric and irrigation purposes. If the dam was built at the most suitable site, it would mean that the temples at Abu Simbel would be submerged. The dam was urgently needed, but there was an international outcry at the possible destruction of the two temples. After years of international discussion, a scheme was evolved whereby the temples were cut out of the cliff and moved up to higher ground in the 1960s.

The house in the photograph that I was holding was at Abu Simbel, in the area that was flooded when the dam was built. All the people living there had to be re-housed elsewhere, since their homes were totally submerged. That is why I said, 'Everybody has gone away. We should not be here.'

The man who lived in that house was a Hajji, a person who had been on the Hajj, or pilgrimage, to Mecca. The drawings on the wall of his home were the record of his journey. Helen had been to Egypt several times and knew the area. The fern-like trees that I described were the trees of Egypt. Later she showed me a photograph of these trees partly submerged; they were just as I had seen them. I had never been to Egypt nor seen photographs of the Abu Simbel temples and so I was amazed at my own accurate description of a place I had never encountered.

The Ancient Wisdom

3

In those days when the wise ones, the Light People, taught the Ancient Wisdom, the Laws of Nature, to the young whom they saw had the light of understanding in their eyes and kindness in their hearts, they had initiation chambers in specially built mounds where, after many years of study, the aspirant to the higher order would come and spend three days alone. These were the three days of ceremonial death when, cut off from the world, the final wisdom was imparted telepathically.

In many religions, the three-day ceremonial death continues to the present day. Christians, for example, celebrate it at Eastertide. For the origin of this we must look to the sky — to the winter solstice, the darkest time of the year, when for three days the sun stands still at its most southerly declination. This is the only time of the year when the light of the sun shines into such mounds, down the long passage and enters the initiation chamber. When it leaves the chamber on the third day, the year has turned and the days begin to lengthen.

Wherever these mounds are found, archaeologists label them 'passage graves'. Yet I know from my time travels that they were not originally graves, but initiation chambers — not places of death, but rather of life. They were used as graves only later, when people had lost their origin of purpose. The archaeologists also call them 'burial mounds' because they find bones in them, but these have accumulated there long after the original purpose of the chamber was forgotten.

To understand these places one must look to the sky, as their Megalithic builders did. They were totally aware of the unity of heaven and earth; they knew of the influences pouring down, affecting all life and all things. This true knowledge has become distorted in the shape of organised religion, which has lost its true roots in the sky, in the planets, the stars, the sun, the moon. Pious platitudes and meaningless prayers have taken the place of the ability to understand and use the Light forces.

To be in one of these mounds at the correct time, to absorb the atmosphere, to dream a little, to meditate, to float with your feelings, brings heaven and earth together more closely than any cleric, performing church ceremonies, can ever do.

Initiation at Newgrange

A site we visited several times was Newgrange in Co Meath. This great mound is about 36 feet high and aligned to the winter solstice. There is a narrow passage, 62 feet long, leading to a central chamber off which there are three small chambers, one at each side and one facing the passage. Thus the whole mound is a circle with a Celtic cross inside it, made up of the central passage and the three chambers. There is a stone basin in each of the small chambers. At the winter solstice, the rising sun shines into the central chamber through a narrow slot between the stones above the entrance to the mound.

It is not possible to meditate alone at this site. There are always people there: bus loads of visitors crowd into it and guides, with scant knowledge of astronomy, tell them it is a passage grave. Astronomy should be a compulsory subject for all archaeologists; without it, they can never understand the original purpose for which these places were built.

We took some photographs at Newgrange, so that I could use these at home to see pictures of what happened there. We decided that at the winter solstice Helen would come to my house for the time of sunrise. I sat in my own armchair, holding one of the photographs we had taken of Newgrange. She was ready to take notes. I prayed for protection as usual, then asked to be shown what happened there at this time of winter solstice sunrise.

I saw a crowd of people. One person came out of the crowd and went forward towards a tall, grey, concave stone near the entrance. As he passed the stone, he pressed his left shoulder and arm against it. He entered the passage and saw something white on the ground, a little way in. (Presumably this was the first light of dawn, just before the sun rose above the horizon.) As he moved along the passage towards the chamber, I heard a voice say, 'Go alone into the circle.'

He entered the chamber, which was filled with a beautiful light, quietly glowing and lovely. Standing in the chamber was what at first I thought to be a pillar of light, then I realised it was a person — a Light Person. The man who had entered held out his hands towards the Light Person in a gesture of welcome. The Light Person acknowledged the welcome, then moved towards one of the side chambers and somehow poured light into the stone basin, leaving a pillar of light standing there. He went to the next basin and the next, each time pouring light into it. He then turned towards the passage, to leave the chamber. As he went I heard the man say, 'Goodbye, Light Friend'.

The man was now left alone. He looked around; the light was still there in the basins, though the Light Person had gone. He moved towards the basin on the left and stood gazing into it, holding out his hands with the palms towards it. He was looking at pictures that had built up in the light; there was also a black spike standing up in the middle of the light column.

I heard a voice say, 'To come. What is to come? The future can be seen in the light.' After a little while, the pillar of light descended slowly into the basin, until it looked like a bright mushroom. The man then bent his body, bowed and went to the centre basin. It, too, was full of light, a lovely pillar shining up, and under it in the basin was a black ball. (In traditional symbolism, a ball can symbolise either the sun or the moon.) He held out his hands towards the light; he seemed to be feeling and collecting it . . .

The pictures suddenly switched off. I waited a while, hoping they would come again. But no, it was over. I was not shown the third basin or what else the man did at the centre basin.

This happened frequently at other sites, too. I was shown so much, but not everything, as if there were secrets that I was not allowed to know or see. Was this regeneration of a solar energy centre? I got the impression that this man was anchoring the energy and he had obviously done it before. Was he an initiate, a priest?

Looking at it in a practical way, it is possible that the basins may have contained water. The sunlight could have reflected off the water and temporarily illuminated some of the motifs decorating the roof and walls, thus in some way giving the priest instructions or guidance. The original purpose of this mound we call Newgrange was not as a burial place. It was a strong energy centre. It was only used for burials many centuries later, by people who did not understand its purpose.

Light Power at Tara

The sun died and was born again at Newgrange. Then, at Tara, it reached its greatest glory. This was one of the most venerated places in ancient Ireland, the seat of priest-kings long before historical times. Later, it became the seat of the secular High Kings of Ireland, when Christianity had replaced the ancient religion.

There is little to be seen there now but simple earthworks, humps and hollows. All the buildings have long since disappeared. They were probably made of wood or wattle and daub. There is one mound, much smaller than Newgrange, with a narrow passage leading to a small chamber.

The day we went to Tara was bitterly cold and windy. We walked around, getting the feel of the site. It was high, with a wide view of open country to the west. Having found a sheltered spot, I settled down to see pictures.

The first thing I became aware of was that it was a warm day, the sun was shining and there was an air of anticipation. People were expected to come across from the west. Looking in that direction I eventually saw them — hundreds of people, streaming across the central plain towards Tara's holy hill. Nearer and nearer they came, expectant and confident, their eyes fixed on the hill.

There were two people on the summit, one in white robes, the other in brown — the priest-king and his assistant. As the people streamed up the slope, the priests raised their arms towards the sky, invoking heaven for the gift of light.

Over the hill a great ball of light appeared. The priests continued to invoke the light — they seemed to be trying to draw it down. Then it came — a mighty pillar of golden light stood on the hill. It appeared to be pouring out strength to the people. It was their yearly birthright sent from heaven, the golden light to feed the soul of Ireland and its people. They soaked it up and were strengthened with power.

All that part of the picture was very clear. Then other vague images came floating in, as if they were very far away in time and not easily focused. There was a lovely valley bathed in golden light. There was a grey stone standing on the right. There was something shaped like a ship; it contained water and had patterns on the sides — squares, wavy lines and circles. It appeared to have something to do with gold. There was a bearded man in white who had some association with the ship. But this was all vague and disconnected. Then the pictures faded completely.

What was all this about? Here was a third site where light was being used for a definite purpose. At the Piper's Stones in Wicklow, the stones seemed to generate light which could be sent up for protection. At Newgrange, the stones apparently stored solar light. And at Tara, the light was brought down for the people to absorb.

Was there any connection between this use of light on a grand scale and the ancient manuscripts, such as *The Book of Kells*, in which some of the illustrations are so fine with such minute detail there is no known drawing instrument available at the present day capable of doing such delicate work. The magnetic field around each person can be seen as light by those who have got psychic vision; could this light have been focused and used in those ancient times?

We sat in the mound at Tara one August evening, waiting for the rising of the full moon. I was not deliberately 'travelling' that evening; no one was talking, no one was taking notes. It is a small mound with a short passage. We sat right back against the end wall. Some of the diagrams on a stone at the side of the passage appeared to indicate the phases of the moon. 'Decorative motifs', as the earth-bound archaeologists call them, can frequently be related to celestial motion.

Our objective that evening was to see if the full moon would shine directly into the mound, onto the back wall, as it rose over the horizon. We had tried to do this in July, but there had been clouds that evening, some of them right on the eastern horizon covering the rising moon. When the clouds cleared, the moon was too high in the sky to know if it would have shone into the passage. But this evening, the sky was clear and the air balmy. We wandered around the site in the twilight, since there was some time to spare before moonrise. The humps and hollows of the earthworks seemed more alive in the half-light than in daylight. One could almost imagine them as inhabited buildings again.

The eastern sky began to get brighter. Soon the moon would be up. We returned to the mound and settled in the back as the light got stronger each minute. Then the moon rose over the horizon, inch by inch until at last its enormous disc was framed in the entrance, shining directly into the mound and lighting up the back wall.

We sat entranced, unable to move. I got the distinct impression that visitors would come and we were waiting to greet them. This feeling lasted as the moonlight gradually moved along the back wall, up the side of the passage and withdrew from the mound. As it finally left we came to our senses, stretched our cramped bodies and stood up.

While framed in the entrance, the moon was enlarged as through a telescope. The mound-builders knew how to get a celestial body framed for observation. These superb astronomical observatories were scattered over the land, as mounds, stone circles and standing stones, with such precision that they still function accurately after thousands of years.

Going outside and seeing a normal-sized moon high in the sky seemed something of an anti-climax, as if we had crashed to earth after a trip to outer space. But we had proved our surmise by direct observation — the rising full moon had shone directly into the mound. Investigators unwilling to work outside their nine-to-five jobs can never hope to understand these sites. They would learn more by staying in bed all day and working on the megalithic sites at night — excepting, of course, those oriented to the sun!

The Mystery of Knowth

The great mound of Knowth in the Boyne Valley has been excavated by archaeologists for years. The public are not allowed in, but the site is close to the road and can easily be seen across the hedge. All we could do was to sit there in the car. I would dearly like to get into that mound and really feel it, get to know it. It is slightly higher than Newgrange, but the diameter is less.

However, we decided that though we could not get onto the actual site I would try my time travel to see if the powers-that-be wanted us to know anything about it. What I got was interesting, though I do not understand it all.

First I saw a peculiar, large brown face, like a monkey's face, but it was not a monkey, nor was it human — more a travesty of a face. Then I was in a cave-like place, lit by a dim brown light. I could not see where this light was coming from; it was just a general glow. As I moved forward, I saw a white light coming down on the left and a yellow light coming down on the right. Then the white light appeared to be standing up. I could now see that there were two passages where the lights were. I said, 'It is hard to know which way to go.'

I eventually took the left passage. It was very steep and went down, down, down into darkness. At last it began to brighten and I came into a large cave, or room, full of yellow light that seemed to come from everywhere, but from nowhere in particular. I went to the left, around the room looking at everything. In the centre, a little closer to one end, was a stone table; there were stone stools here and there near the walls and at the table. Opposite the table, cut into the rock of the farthest wall, were two alcoves that looked like seats or places to display pieces of sculpture or floral arrangements.

On the floor to the right of the table was a black, flat cigar-shaped object, about five or six feet long. The light was getting brighter and there was a beam of yellowish light coming down from the right. I referred to this as mental light and also said, 'There is a feeling of green; I don't know what's green. It's pleasant, astral, protective. Don't worry. Ah, now here are people coming in from the left. What are you going to do?'

Dark People came in first and each put something on the table. They all leaned over it, doing something with whatever it was they had put there.

'What are you doing?' I asked them. But as they ignored me, I went over and saw that they were moving triangles around on the table. For what purpose I could not understand, but they were intent on their task.

Something across the room attracted my attention. I looked up and saw two Golden People had arrived and were sitting in the alcove seats. They appeared to be expecting something and were watching the passage. Then it arrived — long and gold and decorated. It seemed to be a great gold sheet, about six feet long and three feet high. It could have been some form of screen since it came between them and the table where the Dark People were.

It gave me an impression of absolute beauty. It was richly decorated, with small black and blue knobs (they may have been gems) and decorations inscribed around them very beautifully. There was something that looked like a gold tulip leaf, about a foot high, at the round end of the screen.

I asked in surprise, 'What are they meant to do with all these things?' Quite suddenly, something that looked like a mountain of snow flopped down on the right and I was out of the cave at once and near a river flowing around a hill.

After that, I was not getting very clear pictures. Somehow I was flitting in and out of the cave. More Golden People had arrived. A triangular design had appeared on the wall at the right, with other decorations. There was a purple light, like it belonged to a king or priest, shaped like a fan, coming down from the triangle.

Then I was outside again in a field where there was what appeared to be a well with flat stones over it. The pictures were gone . . .

Some days later, I was shown a drawing of one of the decorated stones at Knowth. There exactly was the travesty of a face that I had seen first of all the pictures that day. I was amazed, yet gratified to have confirmation of what I had seen. I also learned that the archaeologists had discovered two passages within the mound, just as I had seen them.

It is difficult to know what the scenes I saw were all about. Again, the pictures shut off and prevented me from seeing what was going to happen when more of the Golden People had arrived. This seems to happen all the time. I am shown so much, but not everything. I wonder if it is meant to be like that. Or perhaps it is like going under water, as if I was diving and can only stay down for a certain length of time before I must surface for air. Perhaps this is the same: that it is only possible to go back for a certain period and then one has to return to one's own era. That may be the answer, I'm not sure.

The mound at Knowth may have been used as a teaching centre for very undeveloped people, possibly those who transgressed the law through ignorance and needed special attention. The triangle shape is significant: it symbolises the three-fold nature of the universe. It also indicates possibility, the fusing of body/mind/spirit to make a whole person. These Dark People were moving triangles about on the table in an aimless way. They could not understand nor use the possibility of the triangle; the forward movement to overcome the body/mind duality had not been achieved. They did not have the ability to progress as whole persons, fusing body/mind/spirit.

Gold symbolises enlightenment, the attainment of illumination and spirituality. A screen represents the boundary between the sacred and the secular. Thus, the Golden People I saw may have needed the protection of the gold screen in their work with the Dark People.

Raising the Stones

There is a well-preserved dolmen at Haroldstown in Co Carlow in a field close by the road. It consists of two slightly tilted capstones, which are supported by ten upright stones.

The day we visited the dolmen, there were two horses in the field, who apparently used it as a shelter to judge by the well-trodden interior. When the horses saw us at the dolmen they came over. They were friendly but persistent, and the only way we could get some peace, to see pictures, was to climb on top of the dolmen. We hoped to get information on who built it and for what purpose. But what I saw was quite unexpected.

We were in a wood and I saw 'Dark People' pulling a great long stone through the trees. (When I refer to 'Dark People' and to 'Light People', I am trying to convey the difference between people who are without much knowledge and those who are enlightened. The White People, or Light People, are those who are full of wisdom.) The Dark People pulled the stone to a clearing, a circular place surrounded by trees. A Light Person in a yellow robe was leading them and teaching them what to do. He led them in a complete circle around the clearing, then they left the stone lying on the ground pointed towards the centre.

The people seemed impatient and expectant, but the Light Person told them they must wait for the right time. It was dark in the clearing still, so they must wait. Presently it got lighter. He told them to look up; the moon was coming out of the shadow of an eclipse and the clearing was flooded with the light of the full moon.

They all stood in a circle around the stone, listening to the yellow-robed person. He was teaching them something, but I could not hear what he said. Then he raised his arms towards the stone and made motions with his hands. Slowly the great stone tipped up, and up, and up. No one was touching it, but as he moved his hands, as if encouraging it, it rose to an upright position, then sank into the ground until it was firmly embedded. A trickle of water oozed up around its base. When it was steady, the Dark People scattered and ran away through the trees . . .

There the pictures ended. While I was seeing this, I made several remarks about an eclipse, that the moon helps gravity and this makes it easier to raise the stone.

Here was a fourth example of light being used in yet another way. Somehow the eclipse of the moon was a time when gravity was affected in such a way that a great stone could easily be erected. Was this the answer to the long-hidden mystery of how the stones were moved over many miles and then raised. The people knew how to use light to cut off gravity and so float the stones into position.

I had seen a standing stone being erected, but I did not get any information about the dolmen itself. As we were about to climb down from the capstone, the two horses came back. The pages of my friend's notebook fluttered in a sudden slight breeze and before we realised what was happening one of the horses stretched up, tore a page out of the notebook and swallowed it! Strange things can happen at these ancient sites. Neither of us could remember what had been written on that page, yet it was a continuous narrative without it. Was there something recorded there that the guardians of the dolmen realised they should not have shown me? Did they motivate the horse to remove it totally in the only way it could — by eating it.

Perhaps warring humanity cannot yet be trusted with the

ancient knowledge. We have to learn to live at peace with one another. At the present time, with the whole planet in turmoil, unscrupulous leaders might use anti-gravity, or levitation, to destroy rather than to build.

A Circle of Wisdom

Not far from the Haroldstown dolmen in Co Carlow is a stone circle that we have frequently visited; sometimes on our own, sometimes with friends. It is at Castleruddery in Co Wicklow. Though looking neglected, almost hidden in long grass and with many of its stones lying flat, I feel a sense of friendliness coming from this circle.

It seems to have been more or less a double circle: the outer stones are set up on a bank, while the inner circle is much lower. Some hawthorns grow on the bank and when covered in masses of blossom they fill the air with a glorious perfume. The fairy thorn was very much part of the circle that spring day we visited it with our friends from abroad, guarding its secrets until the time came to reveal them to someone who would understand and appreciate their perfection of purpose.

I went around the circle touching each stone, feeling its response. On the eastern side, shining white in the sunshine, were two great quartz stones; if polished until mirror-bright, they could have been visible reflectors of light away across the country, perhaps to the hills in the distance. Opposite them, across the circle, there was an upright stone on the bank. It was not nearly as large as the quartz stones; its top was rounded and the front was indented with many pock marks. Immediately I touched it I felt it would talk to me. I told my friend about it and we decided to return another day without our present visitors. For today, it was enough that the sun was shining, the air was full of perfume, our three visitors from abroad were happily speculating about the stones and we had brought a picnic with us.

The day the two of us returned was cloudy and overcast; the drizzle of rain came down almost as soon as we settled ourselves against the 'talking' stone. But it did not bother us, we were well wrapped up and had waterproofs to sit on.

I travelled back to a bright warm night, with all the lights of heaven ablaze. It was the sort of night when one could only gaze in wonder at the glory spread overhead, to know that all moved on their pre-ordained courses, influencing life and movement so predictably that people could learn how to use their emanations.

Very soon I realised that this was a teaching place. This circle was a school of cosmic knowledge. A bunch of happy and excited students, led by their teacher, came into view, obviously glad to be together and looking forward to tonight's lesson. As they came into the circle, I saw there was a tall stone in the centre that had not been there before I went back in time. The top of it was pointed and sloping towards the south, as if indicating a direction.

The teacher told his students to look up, to watch the sky, to see the glory spread above them. He said he had brought them there to learn the meaning of these lights and how their influences could be used through the great stones. Each stone was in tune with a light. They would learn to understand the message of the stars and gradually, after many years of study, they would know how to bring down the light and use it for many things. But now they were young and carefree, happy and excited at having been chosen for this special class at night, when many of their fellows were in bed. They wanted to know when they were going to start, why did their teacher delay, when was he going to tell them about the stars?

He told them that he would not be teaching them tonight; greater teachers than he were coming — the Light Teachers who were full of wisdom. They would be travelling through the air and would come down on the ground where the tall stone in the centre was pointing. 'Watch the sky for the Light Teachers,' he told them.

So they watched and waited impatiently, until one of the students called to the others to look. Travelling towards them through the sky was a ball of light; it was coming rapidly nearer and nearer. They kept pointing at it excitedly and asking their teacher many questions.

'Yes, yes', he said, 'it is the wise Teachers who are coming. They are travelling in that ball of light.'

Nearer and nearer it came, looking ever larger as it approached and descended gradually, until it landed outside the circle in the direction that the large centre stone was pointing. The teacher was standing at the centre stone; he appeared to be in some form of communication with the Light Teachers, as if he was somehow using that stone to send and receive a message. Perhaps it was able to emit some form of radar beam that guided the light vehicle to its landing place. Whatever it was, he was certainly using that stone in a knowledgeable way.

Just at that moment, my friend in the brown robe arrived — the friend that nearly always joined me on my time travels. He came hurrying into the circle, smiled at the students and teacher, and hurried out the other side towards the ball of light. As he got to it the Light Teachers emerged, wonderful bright shining people, full of knowledge. Obviously they knew my friend well and were glad he had come to meet them. They came into the circle, their light shining around them, and greeted all there. The students were expectantly happy; they knew from what their teacher had already told them that one day, when they had achieved knowledge, they would also be full of light.

The Great Teachers moved around the centre stone. Three times they encircled it. Then each sat with his back towards the centre stone and faced one of the outer stones of the circle.

The cosmic power, the cosmic light, filled the circle. Each stone was alive, ready to talk; each was tuned into its own celestial body, so that the power could be used through the stone. The students, seekers after the true universal knowledge, were about to learn how to use this power of light to protect and nourish the land and its people. Each Light Teacher beckoned to a student, who moved closer to him — one teacher to one student to one stone. Every stone was different and there were many things to learn. Gently and lovingly, the Light Teachers guided the students to understand the function of their own stone: how to touch it, feel it, listen to it, draw down the light and use the light. Each student understood one stone; together, they understood them all. As players in an orchestra each had their own instrument, a part of the whole group.

The lesson was over. The Great Teachers prepared to leave, saying they would come again on other nights when each student would learn to understand another stone and then another, until after many nights of teaching each would come to understand every stone in the circle. Then wherever they lived across the land each would be a custodian of the powers of light, a guardian of their people. Wherever the stone circles stood, each would have his work to do . . .

This was all clear seeing for me: no hesitation, no haziness in the pictures. It was so obviously a school where the students were taught how to use the powers of light; this time it was the lights from the night sky, the planets and stars that they learned to use.

I was realising now that so much of this ancient craft had been handed down to us over the millennia through astrology. The ancient and sacred science of astrology, as used by priests and doctors and the intelligentsia for the spiritual, physical and intellectual well-being of all people, had become debased and villified as mere superstition when people became materialistic and cut off from their roots in the stones and the sky. It needed to be restored, to be revived in its original form, for it is only with knowledge of both astronomy *and* astrology that we can ever hope to understand the stones.

Interpreting the Symbols

Sometimes what I see is symbolic and needs interpretation. I wanted to know what happened at the summer solstice, at the time of the sun's entry into Cancer, the moon sign. I had a feeling that the outlier at the Piper's Stones in Co Wicklow had a moon connection. It is a large rotund stone, almost six feet high, lying some forty yards outside the circle.

I moved around this stone, touching it with my hands, trying to remember how we used it long ago. Perhaps some day I will remember clearly at all times. But for now I leaned against the stone, absorbing its atmosphere, willing it to talk to me. Then I went into deep meditation.

I was in a wood of young thin trees like silver birch. Bright moonlight was shining through the leaves and a little deer was standing there as if entranced, looking up at the moonlight through the softly moving leaves. It was such a beautiful little spotted deer in a beautiful silver wood.

A beam of light came down behind the deer and somebody with a brown beard came down from the light and stood beside the animal. They seemed to know each other. They both moved forward along a narrow path, with a high cliff on the left. The deer was leading the way, dancing and prancing with happiness. The man was hurrying along behind the deer; he was obviously fond of his little friend, putting his hand on its head whenever he was near it.

They went along the cliff path, down a slope into a saucer-shaped hollow. A brown-robed person was waiting there. I could see both men talking busily to each other, but I could not hear what they were saying. (So often this happens; I seldom hear them.) Then the men and the deer moved towards a tall stone with a sharp top and under a stone entrance to a passage that went down and down, until they came out beside a bush with the cliff behind it.

The pictures then became confused. There was a mist swirling and swirling around, as if to gather itself together, and light was coming in from the right. The mist eventually did gather itself together and made a shape like a scallop shell or a fan. Mauve light poured down against the stones. A white horse with a long tail appeared going towards the light. Then the pictures stopped.

I came back to the present, wondering what I had been prevented from seeing. The moon influence still seemed strong. Diana, the moon goddess, had sent her deer and, at the last moment, her white horse. Was she following, but not wanting to be seen? Was there to be some ceremony I was not permitted to witness? The mauve light was preparing an atmosphere for ceremonial.

The shell is the badge of the pilgrim. Silver birch trees denote the life of the cosmos, generative and re-generative. They are symbols of immortality and absolute reality linking the three worlds. The trees I saw were young, so perhaps their full significance is not yet developed in my mind. I have seen silver birch several times on my time travels.

The carvings on the ancient stones at Newgrange and other sites still need interpreting. In August 1799 near Rosetta in Egypt, an ancient stone was discovered that eventually led to the deciphering of the Egyptian hieroglyphic writing. It was in three sections — Egyptian hieroglyphics on top, Demotic characters next and Greek at the base. Perhaps one day such a stone will be found in Ireland, that will lead to the deciphering of the carvings on the stones at our ancient sites.

Light on *The Book of Kells*

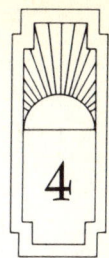

I feel that a grid of energy (white stream, ley line, call it what you will) passes through my house, particularly in the corner of my living room where there is an old chaise longue. Years ago I picked this up at an auction room for a very small sum, as nobody else wanted it. Since then it has more than earned its keep as a place of rest and inspiration, and as a place for my time travels.

The Book of Kells has always fascinated me. I have a small copy of the book, but an artist friend offered to lend me his much larger copy, but only for a week; he remarked at the time that there were no modern drawing instruments capable of doing such fine, minute decorations.

For the whole week, I absorbed *Kells* — every page, every detail. I marvelled at the patience and dedication and craftsmanship of the artists and at their sense of humour that could twine the limbs of people and of animals into weird contortions, putting a surprised look on their faces that seems to ask, 'How am I going to get out of this mess?' On pages of script, someone with a comical imagination has inserted a fish, a hen, a peacock, a cat, as if to lighten the intensity of the work. I wanted to know more about these artists.

One day, while seated on the old chaise longue in the corner, I became totally aware of the earth revolving on its axis. I was watching the morning sunshine move across the wall. It was then I became aware of the earth revolving on its axis.

It was an amazing awareness that I had never felt before, and I still feel it — that I am on this moving planet, it's rolling over, I'm rolling over with it, moving through space, circling the sun and rolling over at the same time.

I turned on the tape recorder, put my hand on *The Book of Kells* and asked to be shown how this book had been made, painted, written. How was it done? What did they use? Did they have special drawing instruments? Did they use light? Here is the transcript of the tape recording made that day.

I see a sort of grey cloud and it looks like silver rain coming out of the cloud, and a wing on the left. Sunshine — the sun is coming up above the cloud and to the right there are golden streaks, like streaks of golden rain going down to the right. The silver rain is going down to the left. There is a green field, and under the cloud on the right there are people; people on the left, too. The people are somehow receiving the spikes of golden rain that are coming down. People on the left are receiving spikes of silver rain that are coming down. There is something brown there in the middle. They are turning now — both lots of people are moving off to the right with what they have collected.

They are going to the right, people with the gold sort of rain first, people with the silver sort of rain going after them, going over to the right. There is something brown, what is it there? A dark brown bit of something, there on the right under their feet. They keep going on, walking towards the right; they are walking through sunshine, going towards a green path, towards a deep kind of path that seems to go down to a sort of tunnel. The path has gone deep, sides high, and they are going down this path in single file towards the tunnel, like a cave, I think. They're going in towards this, through this sort of tunnel, more like a cave, but I don't think it is a cave. And they're going in through, into a room.

They have come into a room and there are other people there; they've been waiting for them, they're welcoming them and they are happy with what they've got. The people with the golden rain are putting it on a table — it's a wooden table, a long wooden table. The bowl of golden rain is on the table now. Where are the other people? Are they coming? Yes. The golden rain is put on the left side of the table, left end of the table. The people with the silver sort of rain — they're coming now; they're a bit behind the others, they're coming now later. They're going over, they're putting it on the right end of the table. The other people there are glad to see them; they've been waiting for them and they're glad to see them now.

They are looking into the bowls and seeing what these are. They're extraordinary things: they're like . . . it's difficult to describe what is in the bowls. The people are looking at them and lifting them up; they're like — something like needles, or pins without heads, silver ones, something as if the silver was in the gold, I think. They're little torches — they're like little torches, little lights. They somehow pick one up, like a little light, like a little torch. Something about a cauldron, I don't know what that is. Little gold torches, little silver torches.

They lift the bowl off the table and put it on the floor, under the end of the table. That's the little gold torches. Somebody has gone down to the other end of the table and lifted off the bowl of silver torches and put it on the ground under the table at that end. Now they are sitting down and they have got pages. Sitting down at this long narrow table with a long bench; and they're sitting down on the bench.

Now they all seem very happy, now they can get on with their work. Yes, they had run out of little torches and things waiting for them. They could only do big work while they were waiting. Now they have the little torches they can do the little work. They've got their sheets; there's four of them sitting on that bench with their sheets of drawing in front of them.

I feel that my friend in the brown robes is standing in the background, behind these people who are sitting down. I'm standing here facing them. I think my brown friend is over there, it looks like him. Yes, it is, that's good. Now let's see. Two people in the middle of the bench are writing; they have pages of writing and they are carrying on with this writing.

The one at each end has got — ah yes, I've moved round and I'm standing behind them, I can see what they are doing much better. Yes. The man down here, he's on my right now, has got the bowl under his end of the table. It is the one with the little gold torches. He has got a page with a drawing on it; there's lots of gaps in that drawing. Now he is bending down, he's picking up a little gold torch, he is using it to do his little drawings, filling in the gaps in part of the drawing — a wing of some kind, a wing I don't know. He has bent down under the table again, picked up a little gold torch, now he's up again. Let's see, I can see over his shoulder. My brown friend has come over to me; now what are they doing, what is he doing?

Somebody else has come in now and he is looking at the man across the table, the artist who is doing the drawing. The artist has looked up at the other man, he is telling him something. What's he telling him? They are having a good chat anyway, can get on now with the drawing, so he is. Yes, now that other man has moved away and the artist is getting on with it. They all seem so happy.

It's extraordinary! With that little torch, he is doing sort of funny little lines on the picture, some little lines, very fine little lines, filling in all these little decorations, all the very fine little decoration things; his little torch is doing it. Extraordinary! He can do this quite quickly, round there, round there; and it's all these funny little designs, the interlacing designs that he is doing. And right down the side of that page the little torch seems to be able to draw these decorations, the interlacing decorations, over and under — yes, that would be it, he is doing some sort of round thing at the corner. He has come up, straightened up his shoulders for a minute; he is saying goodbye to the other man who is going away now.

Now the artist gets back to his work. What's he doing now? Does he want another little golden torch? He is bending down and somehow putting his fingers through the little torches in the bowl. He has picked one up. What is he going to do with this one?

He has gone to the top of the page. This torch is for drawing animals. Drawing animals? Different torches for different things? How can one torch draw signs and another draw animals? I wish he would tell me. I wish my brown friend would tell me. With the little torch, yes, he is up to the top of the page and drawing these funny little animals. Ah, for goodness sakes! Sometimes they look like odd kinds of cats, stretched in all directions. Different animals. A fish. That would be the sacred fish — the Age of Pisces when Jesus was born. He was *Ichthys*, the Sacred Fish . . .

He can draw with two hands at the same time! I don't know how he can do that, but there seems to be something about it; drawing with the two hands at the same time so that he can fit all these twisted animals, lines and things together, over and under. It's extraordinary how he does that! One hand goes under, the other goes over, change, he is winding the animal in, winding the vine around it, winding legs and everything twisted. Drawing with two hands at the same time! That seems amazing! There is some sort of black dot there in front; I don't know what that is.

But, yes, he is talking to the man beside him who is doing the writing. Ah, that's funny! He leans over to the man who is doing the writing and he draws a funny little animal on his page. It looks odd. Yes, he is happy about it. Now the artist has gone back to his own page; and the writer is going on with his writing. They look so happy in their work. There's another fish that has appeared. They love what they are doing. They've got something, I don't know what it is, as if there is a ray of light coming; it is on the floor, really it is the effect that the sun is shining through a window . . .

I saw more than this but, unfortunately, did not realise that the tape had run out until I came back from my journey. These pictures faded so quickly from my memory, like a dream that disappears — they were never written down.

Once again, these extraordinary scenes showed me the importance of light. I feel it is the key to all the Ancient Knowledge. With the modern miracles of laser, X-ray and other lights, humanity will find the key — but only when we can be trusted with it.

A Special Place

There is a place I have seen many times in my time travels, but never yet in my physical body. It is so familiar to me now I feel that I must eventually find it when the time is right for me to do so. There is something there for me, when I have gained enough experience to understand it and be able to pass it on.

Often I have seen this cliff in the forest, a tall cliff going up through the trees, all covered in trailing plants that hide its face. It looks like a high wall of hanging plants, a living curtain of greenery concealing the caves and secret places within it.

Facing the cliff, with arms upraised in an attitude of quiet expectation, is the friend I know so well, dressed in his long brown robe with a cloak thrown back over his shoulders. It is all so familiar — the place, the friend, the quietness, the feeling of sacredness where the innermost sanctuary of the soul could be at peace, a place of natural holiness, where words are unnecessary.

Then the light appears. Gently, quietly, in answer to his expectancy, it comes down through the trees and makes a curtain of light over the green-covered cliff. In places it shines brighter, and these mark the hidden chambers, the secret places where the true wisdom is stored. One spot in particular outshines the rest; it shows him his place of study, the cave that holds the knowledge needed for his present work. He moves forward and gently parts the hanging curtain of living plants at the brightest point of light and enters the store house of knowledge. The green curtain closes back over the entrance; the curtain of light moves up and away. There is nothing to show where he has gone.

The cliff hides its secret places, in the quietness of the trees, the trickle of the little stream flowing by; only the children of nature, the dwellers in the woods, know the ways of the light and the entrances to the caves . . .

Here, apparently, is a place where knowledge is stored. There is no way that I can tell whether it is a library of some sort or whether there are teachers there within the cliff caves. All I know for certain is that my friend has allowed me to realise he is seeking information, but not what the subject might be. He is able to call down the light to his aid. This time it was a guiding light that pointed him in the right direction to find the secret place he wanted. Is this type of light a form of computer that can be used on any site by an initiate to store or retrieve knowledge?

It seems so natural and so simple when I am watching this scene. I have seen my friend by that cliff at other times, but he has not used the light on those occasions. He just stands there quietly, lost in meditation in this lovely peaceful place. I can retreat there in my imagination. Perhaps some day I will find it in reality.

Part II

Our Links with the Cosmos

Cosmic Awareness

6

We are moving into a New Age, the Aquarian Age, when humanity's consciousness is expanding onto a higher level of awareness. People are no longer willing to accept the ingrained precepts of the last two thousand years. When ideas become crystallised in a hard mould, the time has come for them to be broken down, to make way for a fresh reality to emerge. We are leaving the age of pious sentimentalism, the age of pious martyrdom, self-abnegation, spiritual hypocrisy, the wickedness of the Inquisition and of the Crusades, the sanctimonious horrors of burning at the stake those psychic people who spoke the truth.

The whole planet is in turmoil as the last horrors of the Age are being played out — through revolutions, terrorism, murders, torture, bombs, kidnappings, hijackings, drug addiction, alcoholism and rampant sexual aberration.

This total and vicious rejection of all the old ideas is the birth pangs of the coming New Age. Our planet Earth is in the labour ward, about to give birth. It is a difficult labour and needs the skills of experienced hands and minds to bring it safely through and guide it from its first helpless and tottering efforts, to get it firmly on its feet.

In this New Age, spiritual awareness will come through mental activity. Science and religion will fuse as the one truth. Already people are thinking and questioning everything. The children now being born into the world are different to previous generations; they cannot accept blindly what they are told, but must be given a reason, a proof.

In the midst of all the violence, there are people emerging with a deep spirituality that has nothing to do with organised religion. They have an innate awareness of a common humanity that knows no divisions of age, class, creed or nationality; there is a 'shine' about them. They are to be found in meditation groups, in yoga classes, in astrology classes, in prayer groups. Interested in vegetarianism and natural health, working with Samaritans and other voluntary organisations, they are very much aware of social responsibility.

These are the Light People who have returned to planet Earth. As they multiply, the forces of darkness will be overcome, not by war but by the power of Light. A time will come when they will realise that the ancient Light centres should be restored and used. The stone circles, the standing stones, the dolmens, the mounds — these sites are beginning to interest some of them. But it is too soon yet for them to be trusted with the Ancient Wisdom, the true knowledge of how to bring down and use the cosmic power.

No matter what the sceptics say, there are influences pouring in all the time from the sky. These need to be harnessed and used. Present-day astrology gives one an understanding up to a point, but this is just a beginning. It is the ancient science and art of astrology, as used in olden times by priests and doctors, that will re-emerge some day into human consciousness. People will once again become totally aware of the sky being reflected in the Earth and will come to realise that what is happening up there affects what is happening down here.

This planet is a living entity, just as a human body is a living entity. We know a lot about human bodies — what is good for them and what is bad for them, what builds them and what destroys them. What we now need to re-learn is the anatomy of this planet Earth — what used to be known as Earth Magic. The Earth itself is part of the pulsating Cosmos. Cosmic forces are flowing through the body of the Earth, as through all human bodies. We need to re-learn the understanding of gravity and the natural flow of Earth energies. They are there for us to use.

The Ancient Art of Divination

The water diviner, or dowser, is aware of these Earth energies. Through the movement of a forked stick he or she can find underground water. The gifts of the water diviner have been used for many centuries and recognised by people with no esoteric knowledge.

There are many other forms of divination which have come down to us through the centuries. They are now coming back into human consciousness in a wider area, as people are awakening to the incoming influences of the new Aquarian Age. Divination is found in all cultures, in all times, in all parts of the world. It could be described as an effort to gain information of a mundane sort by means conceived to transcend the mundane. In the context of ancient Latin language and belief, divination was concerned with discovering the will of the gods. In some ancient civilizations there was the sacred Diviner Priest or Priestess, whose concern was for the destiny of the people. The Diviner's function was to foresee calamity in order to forestall it.

Nowadays, however, we no longer restrict the word to that earlier root meaning. Present-day divination is usually concerned with practical problems, either private or public. It seeks information upon which practical decisions can be made. But the source of such information is not conceived as mundane.

In a general way, it could be said that there are three different forms of divination: inductive, interpretive and intuitive. Inductive divination uses non-human phenomena as indications that can be read. Astrology would come under this heading, as would the casting of dice, the fall of an arrow shot in the air and the art of augury, or interpreting omens. In ancient Mesopotamia, augury was associated with burnt sacrifice; the priests watched the rising smoke and the movements of birds, to see if there was an auspicious answer to a ritual query. They frequently examined the liver of the victim and read it in the manner of palmistry; this was known as haruspicy.

Interpretive divination, on the other hand, combines non-human phenomena with human action; the special gifts of the diviner are used to interpret the meaning. The crystal ball, tea leaves, I Ching, Tarot and dowsing are among this type of divination.

Intuitive divination is when the diviner needs no trappings. He or she 'knows' the answer. The dictionary defines intuition as 'an immediate apprehension by the mind without reasoning. Immediate apprehension by sense. Immediate insight'.

I feel that intuition has a lot to do with understanding the nature of time. To me, time is like an ocean within which we exist; we can float forwards or backwards or sideways to get information. The great university of space, with all knowledge, is around us. Past, present and future are there for us to reach into. Each of us may use our own particular method of tapping such information. The more urgent our necessity to get information, the more surely we will get an accurate answer. If we are only 'fooling around', the result is not always accurate.

When your intuition is strongly developed, the information can drop into your mind quite naturally. You 'know' without any effort, without understanding how you 'know'. There is no room for doubt — you are totally aware of truth at that moment. For others, the knowledge will come as a vision, or a day-dream, or at night in what seems to be a dream but may, in fact, be a projection to another place, another time.

Information can come through meditation, by first holding in your mind the question to which you need an answer. Then relax, go into meditation and allow the information to flow through.

Psychometry, or getting information through touch, can help your intuition to function. If it is a person you want to know about, you can hold between your hands something connected with that person: their photograph, their hand-writing or some personal possession. Their shoes are possibly the easiest to work with, as long as they have not been worn by someone else or been repaired since last worn by the owner. Put a hand into each shoe and feel the information flow through your hands.

If it is a place you want to know about, it can be done through a photograph or through something from that place. If you are at a stone circle, there is usually a stone that will 'talk' to you if you put your hands on it. My own method is to touch each stone in the circle to find one that will respond to me; then I sit on the ground with my back touching this stone. It is well to pray for protection, then ask to be shown the ceremony or use of the circle. From a deep meditation I talk about what I am seeing, while a friend writes down what I say.

In all forms of divination, it is essential to switch off your logical mind and just allow the information to flow through from the subconscious mind, from the soul level. Later, you can bring logic to bear on the information you have received.

In the twelfth chapter of St Paul's first epistle to the Corinthians, he wrote to the Greeks about spiritual gifts. The early Church accepted and used these gifts as normal. But nowadays, unfortunately, the Church condemns so much ancient natural knowledge; it seems to have lost its true spirituality. The Bible is full of prophecy, both in the Old and New Testaments.

In Celtic mythology and history we have, among others, the

story of Deirdre. As well as the *Táin*, there are several other versions of this. According to T W Rolleston in *Myths and Legends of the Celtic Race*, 'The Druid Cathbad gazed upon the stars and drew the horoscope of the child; he predicted her great beauty and the death and ruin that would come because of her.'

The Ancient Wisdom is flowing back into humanity's consciousness and awakening the gifts that have been suppressed for many generations, but held in trust by the few enlightened souls down through the centuries.

The ancient art of dowsing is now being used in a wider sense than just for water-divining. As well as the forked stick, the dowser can use a pendulum or angle rods. To be a successful dowser one needs a sense of true humility, a total awareness that one is merely a channel for the information to flow through. A person who is arrogant or selfish cannot dowse.

Dowsing can be used for getting almost any information. For example, you can work out a correct diet, by going over food and avoiding anything to which you might be allergic. It can be used for finding lost objects or missing people, by dowsing, for example, on archaeological sites for dates and information, or over a map for directions. The time will come when a dowser will be called upon by the police to find a kidnap victim or a missing person.

From Pisces to Aquarius

Approximately every 2,000 years our planet Earth moves into a New Age. This is not a sudden happening, but a gradual transition over several generations. For a New Age is new people with a new level of consciousness. Those who are living in a transition period are privileged people; many of them have incarnated as heralds and avatars to bring in the Light that dispels the cloud of ignorance.

At this time we are living in a transition period: the Age of Pisces is fading out as the Age of Aquarius is being phased in. There are Piscean and Aquarian souls in earth incarnations just now; this can tend towards misunderstandings, as the Pisceans can be stuck in the traditions of their Age, while the Aquarians are more open-minded and universal.

The Ages are astronomical facts, not merely wishful thinking or imagination. They are caused by a 'wobble' in the Earth which gives, astronomically, the precession of the equinoxes; the first point of Aries on the ecliptic is moving backwards through the constellations. This often causes confusion between astrologers and astronomers, between the signs of the zodiac and the constellations, because the same names in both sciences do not represent the same parts of the sky.

The ecliptic is the apparent path of the sun around the Earth. We are aware that the Earth moves around the sun, but from Earth it appears to be the other way. If we lived on Mars it would appear to us that the sun moved around Mars. The ecliptic is divided into twelve sections of thirty degrees each, named Aries, Taurus, Gemini, Cancer, Leo, Virgo, Libra, Scorpio, Sagittarius, Capricorn, Aquarius and Pisces. The zodiac is a band extending about eight degrees on each side of the ecliptic; it is sometimes described as the Earth's aura or magnetic field.

The constellations (groups of stars) that form the background to the ecliptic have the same names as the signs of the zodiac: Aries, Taurus, Gemini, etc. Astrologers work with the ecliptic, the signs of the zodiac. Astronomers work with the constellations. Both groups can be arguing at cross purposes, unless each acknowledges the other's priorities.

As well as revolving around the sun and rotating on its axis, the Earth has a third movement called nutation. At some time in our childhood, each of us has probably played with a spinning top and may have noticed that, as it spins, the top is not quite upright — the handle is making a circle in the air. Our planet Earth is behaving in the same way: the north pole is tracing out on the sky a circle of $23\frac{1}{2}$ degrees radius. So that the first point of Aries (the spring equinox) is moving backwards (precessing) through the constellations. It completes the full circle in 25,868 years, then the zodiac signs and the constellations coincide again for a while.

Our present world is in upheaval as people's values change from emotional and mystical Pisces to scientific, intellectual, humanitarian Aquarius. Pisces is an age of religions that teach self-sacrifice, martyrdom, acceptance, retirement from the world, carrying one's cross, piously hoping for the best rather than being practical. Aquarius, in contrast, is much more practical and very group-conscious, a thinker who wants freedom on all levels of experience. On the lowest level are found the revolutionaries who want freedom but who have not worked out in a practical way how to achieve it, nor what to do with it if they get it. So they plant bombs, they shoot, they kidnap, they maim, in many countries all over the world. On a higher level are the wanderers; they are not violent, but seek freedom from the 'rat race'. They wander the world with their back-packs and guitars, getting short-term jobs in each country they visit, maybe spending some time in an Indian *ashram*. They are not quite sure what they are seeking, but are unwilling to settle down in a comfortable conventional career.

On the third level are the deeply spiritual people, many of whom have rejected organised religion; they want freedom to think, to make up their own minds on what is ultimate Truth, rather than have other people's ideas forced upon them.

As the Aquarian Age gradually comes in, there is an increasing humanitarian group-consciousness that is making people aware that they *are* their 'brother's keeper'. It can be seen from the United Nations to local community groups. It is only in comparatively recent years that governments have introduced social welfare; typically Aquarian are Samaritans, Simons, Meals on Wheels, Alone, Alcoholics Anonymous, Wireless for the Blind, Guide Dogs for the Blind and many other humanitarian, non-sectarian groups that have sprung up in recent years. Complementary medicine (formerly known as 'alternative') is coming into its own, as people want freedom from prescribed chemicals that contaminate their bodies. There is the Aquarian interest in healthy eating and vegetarianism, vitamins and minerals, and organically grown food. Twenty-five years ago, there were no vegetarian restaurants or health food shops; now there are many.

Uranus is the ruling planet of Aquarius. It was discovered in 1781 by William Herschel at the time of the industrial revolution, when people's lives were changed by machines. Astrologers know Uranus as the planet of deviation from the normal, for better or worse; it is the planet ruling electrical and magnetic forces, which in the present lifetime has brought in the airplane, radio, television and computer. Uranus rules all forms of 'high tech' and is responsible for rapid changes as the Aquarian Age gathers momentum.

Each Age had brought changes in cults and outlook. About 10,000 BC it was the Age of Leo (the Lion), ruled by the sun; temples have been found with lions' heads carved on them, presumed to be dedicated to sun worship. The Age of Cancer, ruled by the moon, occurred in about 8000 BC; then there were moon cults and moon goddesses. Around 6000 BC was the Age of Gemini (the Twins) when there was a cult of pairs of gods. The Age of Taurus (the Bull) came about 4000 BC and with it the worship of the sacred bull; Taurus also rules solid building, and the pyramids and temples of ancient Egypt, Mexico, and central America date from this time. The Age of Aries (the Ram) was about 2000 BC and brought the cult of the sacred ram. Then came Pisces (the Fishes) — and now it is the time of Aquarius (the Water-carrier).

As above, so below

Our planet Earth is so bound up with the happenings in the sky that no one who has studied the ancient spiritual science of astrology can doubt its value in bringing people to a deeper understanding of themselves — who they are and what they can be in developing their true potential.

Astrology, in its true sense — not the pop version — is an ancient science complementary to dowsing. Astrology is celestial influences coming down; dowsing is terrestrial influences coming up. Both these energies are flowing through our bodies.

There are predictable cosmic periods affecting all life and all things. Every heavenly body has its own rhythm: the Sun, the Moon, the Earth, the planets, all bodies move in such perfect rhythm that their positions in the sky can be calculated for many years in the past or into the future. These are published as a 'Planetary Ephemeris' and are used by astrologers and anyone interested in what is happening out in space.

The Earth rotates on its axis, giving us night and day. It travels around the sun, giving us the seasons. These are predictable cosmic periods. We know there is a twenty-four hour rhythm and a yearly rhythm. We also see the Moon going through its phases as it revolves around the Earth (from New Moon to First Quarter to Full Moon to Last Quarter to New Moon again) and moving in and out of the Earth's shadow at eclipses. The Moon revolves around the Earth, but the Moon with the Earth revolves around the Sun, as also do the other planets. Those nearest the Sun have the shortest cycle.

The planets in order from the Sun are: Mercury, Venus, Earth with its Moon, Mars, Jupiter, Saturn, Uranus, Neptune and Pluto. Some astrologers say that the planets Vulcan and Apollo are still to be discovered.

The cycles in the sky are reflected in the cycles on the Earth. The most obvious cycle is the effect of the Moon on the oceans' tides and on the tides in the human body. Enlightened doctors now know that surgical operations should not be performed at Full Moon, since people bleed far more at this time than at other times. A woman's body is particularly tuned in to the cycle of the Moon.

In the days of the Ancient Wisdom, when people understood the Laws of Nature, every priest and doctor was taught astrology and used it to treat spiritual as well as physical ills. An old anonymous text states, 'The end of the physitian's employment in ye case of ye patient that he may accomplish this with more certainty and facility, astrology is very necessary as the handmaid to attend his and other physicall sciences. First to ye knowledge of what part the disease is in and which cause it comes, you are to remember what parts of man's body are signified by ye twelve Houses and Signs of heaven, by ye planetts and ye position of ye planetts which use the significators in any of the Houses and Signs.'

As the New Age is dawning, the Ancient Wisdom is being infiltrated once more into human consciousness. The White Brotherhood is pouring the forgotten Laws of Nature into those who have ears to hear and minds to understand. In the materialistic ages of the past Truth went underground, but there were always those few enlightened ones who kept the knowledge alive.

Copernicus revived the ideas of Pythagoras, that the Sun was the centre around which the planets revolved, not around the Earth as had been taught erroneously. Kepler discovered the three laws of planetary motion, which contain implicitly the law of universal gravitation, and so laid the foundation for Newton's work on gravity.

Gravity draws things together, cosmic repulsion keeps things apart; though its nature eludes us we know that it works. It maintains a balance. The Earth, the Moon, the planets, all keep to their predictable paths, attracted to one another by gravity, but

1. The aspirant to the Ancient Wisdom would have walked down this narrow passage to the central chamber of the great mound at Newgrange, Co Meath. Here, the knowledge of the ages would have been imparted telepathically to the initiate through the powers of light.

2. The great mound at Newgrange, perfectly aligned to the winter solstice sunrise, was built as a powerful energy centre and initiation chamber for those chosen to learn the Ancient Wisdom. The initiate entered the chamber for the three-day ceremonial death and emerged reborn with the Light of Knowledge.

3. The Piper's Stones in Co Wicklow — the first archaeological site I investigated. The special stone that 'talked' to me is the large standing stone opposite the hawthorn tree, across the circle. Are these stones generators of energy or storage batteries of solar power?

4. The great stone circle at Castleruddery in Co Wicklow is a friendly place. The entrance is marked by two massive quartz boulders, in the foreground here. This double circle was a teaching centre in ancient times, where students learned the secrets of the stones and how to use their power.

5. The dolmen at Haroldstown in Co Carlow was the site where I first saw how the great stones were raised — through the negative effect on gravity that occurs at the time of a lunar eclipse. The purpose of the dolmen itself was not revealed to me.

6. Although I had no prior knowledge of the interior of the mound at Knowth in the Boyne valley, this decorated stone within was the first image that I saw in my time travels there. It appeared to me as a rock carved with a travesty of a face — though not a frightening one.

7. In my time travels, I walked through the great mound of Knowth and discovered two passages within. The one I followed led steeply to a teaching chamber where Light People taught the rudiments of knowledge to the Dark People, the ignorant ones.

8. The hill of Tara, one of the most venerated places in ancient Ireland, was the site of an annual ceremony when the priest-king invoked the light of the heavens to come down and strengthen the people with its life-giving force.

9. This is the only engraved stone at Tara, within the Mound of the Hostages. It is decorated with concentric circles and semi-circles, which may represent the cycles of the sun and moon. (Sadly, it has been defaced by vandals in recent years.)

10. On this page of The Book of Kells, *four signs of the Zodiac are illustrated* (left to right): *Aquarius (The Man), Leo (The Lion), Taurus (The Bull) and Scorpio (The Eagle). These astrological signs also symbolise the Four Evangelists of the Christians — Matthew, Mark, Luke and John, respectively.*

kept apart by cosmic repulsion, so preserving a perfectly balanced motion and avoiding collisions.

There are many emissions pervading the Universe: electromagnetic radiation varies through gamma and X-rays, ultraviolet radiation, visible light (which is a very small part of the spectrum), infrared, microwave and longwave. Our eyes are sensitive only to visible light, the middle octave of this vast range of light. Until radio astronomy began in 1931, astronomers were limited to observations by visible light. But with new knowledge and photography, a whole range of cosmic influences pouring through the Universe has become known. Many of these are stopped in the ionosphere before reaching Earth.

So, the positions of the planets may not be the only factor that makes astrology work. Radiations may need to be taken into account too. Deep esoteric knowledge that has always been with mankind (knowing, without knowing how we know) could be given scientific proof. The many biologists and physicists who are investigating cosmic cycles, eclipses, sun spots, solar eruptions and light waves will eventually prove us right as practical mystics and astrologers in tune with the Universal Forces.

The incoming Aquarian influences of the New Age are making themselves felt in the scientific world today. This hitherto earthbound community is beginning to lift its flat feet off the ground and float a little. Scientists are discovering that solid matter is not as solid as it used to be.

Aquarius is an Air Sign, ruling mental activity, a figure pouring out the Water of Life, representing intuition, from an amphora held on the shoulder. This blend of reasoning intelligence and intuition will link all people through understanding, through mental enlightenment.

The scientist wants to prove everything, but the mystic is aware and so feels no necessity for proof. The New Age ideas being sent down into human awareness by those who have us in their keeping are penetrating the bastions of the 'flat-earthers', who will only believe what they can see and touch. The basic oneness of the Universe is one of the revelations of physics; it is the central experience of the mystic.

Indian astrologers have always set up several charts for each client, involving the symbolism of numerology. First, the Rasi chart shows the natal positions; next, the Navamsa or ninth division chart brings out the symbolism of the number nine, associated with the ideal, with completion, the gateway to fulfilment; then, the Panchamsa chart brings out the symbolism of the number five, the putting together of form and matter, thus to create an idea and bring it into manifestation; and so on through the numbers, depending on the immediate needs of the client who is looking for guidance.

In Western astrology, John Addey has come up with the theory of harmonics in astrology, bringing the harmony of the spheres down to mathematical graphs and using the symbolism of numerology in interpretation, much as the Indian astrologers apply it. This system may help to widen astrologers' understanding and perhaps overcome the, at times, somewhat materialistic readings that are given to people who are functioning on a higher awareness and to whom a materialistic interpretation does not apply. Addey's work shows that 'all astrology is based on the harmonics of cosmic periods'. The harmonic chart explains the numerological reasoning behind the ancient theories.

Quantum physics and Eastern mysticism are today finding common ground. Both say there is no solid matter, that all is movement and rhythm. The eternal dance of Shiva on the Earth and quantum physics both agree that all is rhythmic motion. Fritjof Capra's book, *The Tao of Physics*, is an exploration of the parallels between modern physics and Eastern mysticism. As a scientist and student of T'ai Chi, Capra has studied and brought together these apparently opposing views and shows that the continuous cosmic dance underlies the basis of all things.

The I Ching, astrology and Jung's theory of synchronicity are all based on the knowledge that 'whatever is born or done this moment of time has the qualities of this moment of time', as Jung himself said. Einstein's objective was to show that all things, from the atom to the stars, obey the same universal laws.

New Age Psychology

7

From orthodox 'churchianity' to esoteric psychology and occult teaching can be a shattering experience, shaking the very foundations of the normal Church-going Christian who has blindly accepted creeds and dogmas without thought or question. Daily reading of the Bible at a superficial level never leads to the deeper esoteric meanings behind such words as 'Did this man sin, or his parents, that he was born blind?' Quite unaware of reincarnation, people never think to query how a man could sin before he was born.

For a psychic person, born with an innate knowledge of reincarnation and a continual awareness of God in everything, it is the answer to all the questions that have never been satisfactorily answered and also to questions that have never been put into words, for fear of being called 'un-Christian'.

Reincarnation is the slaking of the thirst for Truth, the re-learning of the knowledge gained in previous lives and temporarily forgotten. It is the unfolding of the soul from sleep, as the Light of Truth shines in once more. It is the true knowledge that God is a God of Love and Light and Power. The crippled, ill, deformed bodies, the sorrow and suffering, the tragedies and bitterness — these things are not inflicted on humanity by a vengeful deity. Souls choose to incarnate to gain experience of various kinds — some to experience lives of suffering, others lives of joy.

Reincarnation is the cultivation of love and the brotherhood of man, the realisation of the One Soul of which all souls are a part. It is the ability to meet at soul level, regardless of the age or creed or class of the bodies which the souls are temporarily inhabiting.

It is in this New Age setting that astrology has once more taken its rightful place as the science of the correlation of each living soul with the Universe. The astrologer thinks of the Universe as a whole, summed up by Hone as 'a constantly moving relationship between the very large moving objects in it, such as the Sun, the

Moon and the Planets, and the small moving objects, such as human beings and animals'.

Through the law of analogy, 'as above, so below', the cosmic processes and the nature of the cosmic principles are indicated in the functions, structure and characteristics of a human being. They serve as signposts along The Path, where future signposts may be found.

To all seriously minded astrologers, it is a matter of much gratification that in some modern translations of the Bible, the word 'astrologers' is used instead of 'wise men'. See, for example, Matthew Chapter 2 in the *New English Bible* or in *No Greater Love*.

The birth of Jesus heralded the coming of the Age of Pisces (the Fishes). The occupation of several of His apostles was as fishermen, but they left their nets and followed Him and He made them 'fishers of men'. Again, during the persecution of the early Christians, a rough drawing of a fish's head was used among them as a secret sign.

As Pisces fades out and the Age of Aquarius now takes its place, the seeds that were planted almost 2000 years ago are beginning to sprout and some to blossom. The gospel of love and brotherhood is slowly but surely becoming a reality. Aquarius, the water-carrier, is pouring out the Living Water, so that we might have life and have it more abundantly. World consciousness is beginning to transcend nationalism; within this century many movements have begun that cut across national boundaries and bring people with common interests together, in work, in hobbies, in social welfare in its broadest sense.

In this New Age, we will see astrology being used as a normal fact of life. Birth times will always be noted and parents will have birth charts cast for each child (as some enlightened parents already do). It will then be seen where the child's abilities lie and provision can be made for the type of education and opportunities suitable to the child's personality.

In forming partnerships, whether in marriage or in business, a comparison of birth charts will show whether the people concerned are compatible and likely to succeed. In this way, much unhappiness will be eliminated from the world. The coming in of the Aquarian Age will bring a whole new concept of life.

New Thoughts on Ancient Knowledge

There is nothing new under the sun. What we do nowadays has been done many times before. Going back through thousands of years the same customs have been carried on under different names.

There is a basic inner core of Truth underlying all religions and it has been passed down from age to age through the enlightened souls who can see beyond the outer trappings. (Much organised religion has, unfortunately, become so immersed in outer show and bickering between denominations that it has lost this inner Truth.) It is the Ancient Wisdom, or Ageless Wisdom, that connects humanity with its source — the understanding that all is one, that all is interconnected. Many of the poets understood this: Francis Thompson, Wordsworth, Yeats and others were aware of a common interconnecting thread joining all things, from the minutest atom to the largest star.

There is an interwoven pattern where all is one — where the cycles in the heavens are reflected in the cycles on this planet Earth. The Hermetic maxim, 'as above, so below', shows the macrocosm reflected in the microcosm. Everything that is happening up there, that is happening all around us, has threads of energies connecting all things, all people. It is through these pulsating threads of energies that we can tune in and pick up information by whatever method we choose to use.

We are each born into this life with our own pattern, which is part of the great cosmic pattern with which we are in tune. In ancient times, people identified with the source of all things. They were in tune with the Laws of Nature, in tune with the Cosmos; they had a natural understanding of what was seen to be happening in the present and of what was repeated at intervals.

If we think of ourselves, our human bodies, as upside-down plants, our roots going up towards the sky, with the vital forces of the cosmos passing through us all the time, we get a realisation of ourselves as part of a great universe, in tune with the whole of creation.

As we are now moving into a New Age, we are experiencing a great resurgence of the Ancient Wisdom that has been innate in all people in all times. But it lay dormant during the materialistic and scientific years when humans became drunk with power and vain with assumptions that it was within their power to control all the Laws of Nature.

One of the ancient arts that is now becoming part of our present awareness is astrology. It has survived through thousands of years with people of all races and is presently emerging from a dark period of several centuries. During that time, it was debased and scorned as mere superstition, as humanity's scientific knowledge developed and put an increasingly materialistic valuation on life. Astrology, the divine science, is the most sacred and ancient language in the world; each of the glyphs used has a deep spiritual meaning.

Today, we are experiencing the birth pangs of a New Age. The whole world is in turmoil. We are on the threshold of a new era when, according to the symbolism of the Zodiac, the long hidden Truth will be revealed. Approximately every 2200 years, the influence of the Zodiac pours through a new awareness. We are moving into the Age of Aquarius, symbolised by the figure pouring out the water of life, when spiritual awareness will arise through mental enlightenment. The Earth is passing from the Age of Pisces to the Age of Aquarius, from the Sign of the Fishes to the Sign of the Man.

Jesus was born at the last transition period, when the Age of Aries (the Ram) was passing out and the Age of Pisces (the Fishes) was entering. He was welcomed by the shepherds, the representatives of Aries, as the Lamb of God. He chose fishermen as His apostles, making them 'fishers of men' representing the New Age of Pisces. He was born in the country that is the meeting place of east and west.

All the truths of Christianity stem from a much older tradition, when humanity was aware of its roots in the sky. It is the religion of the Age of Pisces and all through Christianity runs this symbolic thread of the Fishes. Jesus was known to his followers as *Ichthys*, the sacred fish. Fish with bread and wine was the sacramental meal of the ancient Mystery religions. We find in Christian art the ancient tradition being carried on — the Eucharist is represented by the sacramental fish with wine and a basket of bread.

In the National Gallery of Art in Dublin is Titian's wonderful painting *The Supper at Emmaus*. Jesus, in the centre of the group, has broken the bread; near His left hand is the fish and beyond it is the wine. Presumably He was an Essene, making Himself known through the sacramental meal of the ancient Mystery religion. Instead of painting a halo around Him, Titian has shown the light coming up from the head 'chakra'; the master painter was aware that The Master's head centre would be open.

The days of the week are each named after the planetary God whose hour started the day at sunrise: Sunday is ruled by the Sun, Monday by the Moon, Tuesday by Mars (*Mardi* in French), Wednesday by Mercury (*Mercredi* in French), Thursday by Jupiter (*Jeudi* in French), Friday by Venus (*Vendredi* in French), Saturday by Saturn.

Friday is the day of Venus, the goddess of love and beauty; the planet Venus is exalted in the Sign of Pisces. Friday is the day when fish was eaten in honour of the goddess. The eating of fish on Friday has been continued in the Christian tradition, though the meaning has been changed to that of fasting, because of Good Friday. Early Christians used the fish as a sign of recognition among themselves; they traced it in the dust as their symbol and used it on their tombstones in the catacombs at Rome and elsewhere.

Right through all religions from time out of mind runs the idea of three days of ceremonial death. The would-be initiate into the Ancient Mysteries went through the narrow passage into the initiation chamber, where for three days he was dead to the world but alive to the sacred knowledge that was being telepathically impressed on his mind. On the third day he came forth, reborn from his ordeal, full of the Light of Knowledge, ready to take his place among the teachers and caretakers of his people.

For the origin of these three days we look to the sky, to the winter solstice, to the darkest time of the year, when for three days the sun stands still at its most southerly declination. This is the only time of the year when the light of the sun shines down the long passage and enters the initiation chamber at Newgrange and elsewhere around the world. When it leaves the chamber on the third day, the year has turned and the days begin to lengthen. Its entry into Capricorn is the start of its return to the northern hemisphere.

From this we can see the importance of the number three in all religions. The power of three is universal: the world is heaven, earth, water; mortals are body, soul, spirit; there is birth, life, death; past, present, future. There are innumerable trinities of gods and goddesses; Christianity has Father, Son and Holy Spirit.

In pre-Christian Celtic religion, there was Morrigan, Macha

and Badh, the triple goddess, the three-in-one young woman, mother and old woman. There are the three Brigids and others. In Qabalism there is the trinity of male, female and uniting intelligence. In Greek, there is the trinity of Persephone, Demeter and Hecate.

In the heavens, there are three great cosmic crosses: the Cardinal cross, the Fixed cross and the Mutable cross. The Fixed cross is comprised of the four fixed Signs of the Zodiac:

AQUARIUS	LEO	TAURUS	SCORPIO
The Man	*The Lion*	*The Bull*	*The Eagle*
Matthew	Mark	Luke	John

These are the symbols of the four Evangelists, used in *The Book of Kells* (the four Gospels written in Latin) and in *The Book of Armagh*, *The Book of Durrow* and *The Lichfield Gospels*.

Before the coming of Christianity, we had our own four Great Festivals in Ireland: Imbolc on 1st February, Bealtaine on 1st May, Lughnasadh on 1st August and Samhain on 1st November.

Someone once described we Irish as 'pagan Christians' and there seems to be a lot of truth in this. What are we celebrating at Hallowe'en and All Saints? Are we not, in truth, celebrating Samhain, when the doors of Fairyland are opened and we can move easily through the thin veil between the worlds — the time between times. Or on 1st February, when as Christians we celebrate St Brigid of Kildare, is our folk memory recalling the Festival of Imbolc, ruled over by the great triple goddess, Brigid?

The cult of the goddess is strong in Ireland, though now thinly disguised as the Virgin Mary. Mary's title, Queen of Heaven, is one of the titles given to the Egyptian goddess Isis. Another title, Stella Maris, is also ascribed to the Egyptian goddesses Sothis and Hathor.

As the feminine principle is becoming stronger in the world, so the cult of the Mother Goddess is likely to increase. We have many holy wells in Ireland; these represent the feminine principle, the issuing from the womb of the Great Mother, the Great Goddess. Celtic mythology is full of female deities. There is, for example, Niamh of the Golden Hair, the Goddess of the Land of Eternal Youth, and there is Anu, the Goddess of Plenty, after whom two mountains in Kerry are named — the Paps of Anu.

The Ancient Science of Astrology

As humanity goes up and down the spiral of existence, looking for a meaning to life through the same ideas under different names, there is a resurgence of the Ancient Wisdom into our awareness. Many people are now seeking a meaning to life and finding signposts along the path through the study of the ancient science and art of astrology.

It takes a minimum of three years study to become a qualified astrologer. These pages can only serve to scratch the surface of a vast body of knowledge that goes back into the mists of time. It has always been with us, all over the world. It stems from humanity's desire to identify with the source of all things, to be in tune with the ordered universe, to understand what is seen to be happening now and what is repeated at intervals. Ultimately, it stems from our desire to understand ourselves and how each one of us fits into the Divine Plan.

In the old days, the nights were dark and the sky was visible. Present-day city-dwellers take as normal the bright lights in streets and buildings that obliterate the night sky, making them unaware of nature's timetable overhead.

The dawning awareness of ancient mankind identified closely with all the natural happenings of nature: the rising and setting of the sun by day, the waxing and waning of the moon by night, the cold of winter and the warmth of summer, the seasons as they came and went. The cutting off of the light of the sun during a solar eclipse, or of the moon during a lunar eclipse, probably caused terror among the people until, after many generations, they came to understand what was happening. Then they set up great stones to mark the events in the sky, so that they would know in advance what to expect. With these first celestial observatories, they could then predict the motions of the heavenly bodies.

Astronomy and astrology were originally the same science, but as stronger and stronger telescopes were invented astronomers concentrated on scientific observation, while astrologers continued to bring astronomy down to earth and relate it to people. In the old days, doctors and priests used astrology to get a basic understanding of their patients' problems, both on a physical and a spiritual level. They knew that people were tuned in to the cosmos, that what was happening in the sky was reflected on earth in people, in animals, in plants and in the tides.

To calculate an accurate birth, or natal, chart it is necessary to have the time, date and place of birth, by latitude and longitude. If the time is not known or only approximate, a dowser who is used to this work can find it.

The birth chart is the blueprint of one's life. It shows the energies that flow in a person's magnetic field. At a new-born baby's first breath, it takes into its body the vibrations of that day and that time, at that latitude and that longitude. The chart shows the person's tendencies and potentials, possible problems and latent abilities. It is like a hand of cards that has been dealt out for this life: here is what you have got, but you have free will as to what you are going to do with it. You are not totally 'fated' to be or to do anything.

The birth chart can be likened to a total psychological assessment of a person. The astrologer can explain the chart to a client by comparing it to a road map — the circumstances that you will be meeting in this life, some roads that are difficult and bumpy and need to be mended, others that are easy and smooth to travel on. Life's journey is made so much easier to cope with when you can read the map.

The chart has three components: the Planets, the Signs of the Zodiac and the Houses. The Planets, of which there are 10, are *what* you are doing; the Signs (12) are *how* you are doing it; and the Houses (12) are *where* you are doing it. A Planet could be in any House and any Sign, depending on when and where a person was born. For each individual's chart, all these elements have to be read and synthesised into a coherent analysis, in a totally personal way.

You may well ask, what is an astrologer? What does he or she actually do? Is he or she just a fortune-teller? The answer is, it depends on the type of astrologer you consult. Some are in it only for the money they can make out of it. But a dedicated, spiritually minded astrologer is a counsellor and friend who will give as much time and consideration to each person as is needed. There would be no such thing as limiting a worried or an anxious person to a certain length of time. The astrologer can see the client's basic problems in the chart and so can encourage the client to recognise them and talk them out.

This is where an astrologer can score over a psychologist. They have to question and probe the client, to try and find the genuine basic problem (rarely the one the person is talking about). But the astrologer, through the birth chart, can see the client as a whole, with all their positive and negative traits, with pointers to the possibilities for overcoming their problems.

Some enlightened psychologists are using astrology in their work today, as are a few doctors. The physical body is shown in the chart, from Aries ruling the head right through to Pisces ruling the feet; indications of possible weak areas can be seen and preventative action taken.

I sometimes wonder how many patients in hospitals for mental illness are genuine psychic people, born into materialistic families, who have never had the opportunity to develop their gifts and who have been 'written off' by ignorant people as 'queer and looney'.

As well as the natal chart, there are other charts that can be set up. Some clients find it helpful to get a progressed chart each year; this shows the present trends in the life, how the inflowing energies are affecting the natal chart, so giving indications as to the best action to be taken at certain times.

Charts can also be set up for the 'birth time' of countries or for the re-birth of a country that has gained its freedom from occupation by a foreign power. Thus, a chart for Ireland can be compiled that works accurately through progressions and transits, based on the rebellion that began in Dublin on Easter Monday, 24 April 1916 at 12 noon Dunsink Time.

There are also charts for events, such as the New Ireland Forum, the Anglo-Irish Agreement, the setting up of a new company or an amalgamation of existing companies. There are many clients who ask an astrologer to choose a suitable time and date for an event to be held.

Unfortunately, there are people who debase the ancient science and art of astrology by writing 'star sign' rubbish in newspapers and magazines. I have been interviewed by some of these, many of whom are not qualified in astrology, have never studied the science and may not even have seen a birth chart.

Blueprints

Each of us is born into planet Earth with our own blueprint for this incarnation. As astrologers, we can see this blueprint in the birth chart. Clients come to us with their many problems and dis-ease brought on by their departure from this life pattern. Life takes on its true meaning when the client is shown the path indicated in their chart; then they understand that so many of their problems are brought on themselves by trying to be what they are not meant to be.

Many psychic people and New Age people who are born into materialistic families suffer stress illnesses in this wrong environment. When they meet with a dedicated astrologer who sees in their birth chart what they truly can be and guides them to meet like-minded people, then their illnesses fall away. They realise they are not 'queer'; they discover there are many others in the world who also see something beyond the outer trappings of materialism.

How could we doubt that there is a reason and structure to life? Since we accept that we can work with these guidelines in the chart, we are not alone in our work. Each life is a fountain of energy; there is law and order in a constant state of movement and change. Evolution re-creates and re-forms at a higher attunement, every structure responds, but illness and dis-ease can block the response; the natural response becomes the healing action as soon as the atmosphere is right. We can suggest that they allow love to flow in and forgive themselves, forgive God, forgive all.

Out of the workshop of nature is the fantastic potential for creation. Each form is linked to its own blueprint: the buds come out of the bare branches, the leaves appear in their own patterns, the beauty of the butterfly emerges from the caterpillar's chrysalis. Each responds to its own blueprint, as drawn by the hand of God.

It is when man interferes with the divine pattern that things go wrong. Artificial fertilizers interfere with the balance of nature. The herbs and wild flowers that cattle eat instinctively when they are aware of their bodies' need for healing are disappearing because of unnatural chemicals on the land, so that instead of having the natural herbs available to restore their blueprint, we find the farmer and the vet injecting chemicals into their bodies.

This, in turn, can upset the blueprint in humans who are so lacking in knowledge and compassion for all life that they are stupid enough to eat these unfortunate animals.

The divine pattern can be drawn into places. There is the right place to invoke the situation, the powers, a great flame on the earth linked to the elemental powers. The power is neither good nor bad; it can be used either way. Many spiritual centres are built on power points by people who are guided to provide a Light Centre; they hold the elements. But where the energy is abused, it brings destruction. There are grids and power zones of energy that surround the earth in mysterious ways. They seem to tap the energy that is at the sun within the earth and these join with the great forces from the sky; together at certain points they can establish potentially a great energy area, a great vortex point, a great beautiful solar flame. The ancient stone circles and spiritual centres were built at these sites, as were some of the early Christian churches before the knowledge was forgotten by them.

Life is for living, we use our own sense of balance in responding to people; we are in the Essene tradition of joining to a natural sense of attunement a wholesome, clean-feeling atmosphere.

Time and Light

Are time and light the same thing? The light from a star takes thousands of years to reach our planet Earth. The light we see now from that star left it millennia ago. If we could travel along that beam of light, we would be travelling back in time; all the history of that star is stored on that light beam, as on a strip of photographic film.

So with the light reflected from our Earth — it travels out in time and space. Our history is out there, stored on our Earth beams for all to see, but accessible only to those who have the gift of time travel. A visitor from outer space could pick up the whole story of planet Earth while travelling towards us on our light beam.

Is this what is known as the Akashic record? Is it a strip of film on a beam of light? Is it not a book at all? Has each of us got our life history of many incarnations stored out there for ever? Is this why a person with no particular visionary gift can see people or happenings of another age quite unexpectedly, 'out of the blue', because there may have been a thunderstorm or gale out in space that upset a light beam in such a way that it sent a temporary flash of history back to Earth?

When space travel around the galaxy becomes the normal way of going on holidays, perhaps the historians of that future time will pick up the true facts out there and not have to rely on books, each written from a particular point of view.

A beam of sunlight enters Newgrange at sunrise on the winter solstice. A beam of sunlight enters my home, also at noon, on the winter solstice. The sun is so low in the sky that it shines through my hall door, then a beam of sunlight goes down the long narrow passage and enters the diningroom at the back of the house.

At the summer solstice noon, the sunlight enters that room again, but by a different route. Then, it is so high in the sky that it is above the roof of the house next door and can shine in through the window.

You might say that this house is 'one up' on Newgrange — the beam of light arrives here twice a year.

As long as the sun shines, I need never be at a loss to know the time, though every clock in the house may have stopped. It is exactly 12.15 when the sun beams down the passage and enters the room; at 12.35, it withdraws back down the long passage. This is clock time (Greenwich Mean Time). But the true local time — sun time — is 25 minutes later than GMT: 12.25 clock time is noon by the sun.

When I nearly died, I went down a long passage and saw the Light. It happened like this. I was a young married woman with a little daughter. For some time I had not been well. It was coming up to Christmas and we were going to stay with my parents for the holiday. After the first few days, I was so ill I had to go to bed. The doctor was called in; he diagnosed pneumonia. That was in the days when pneumonia was regarded as a fatal illness and very few people pulled out of it.

However, penicillin had just been discovered and hailed as the miracle drug, the cure-all. Obviously it was the answer to my problem — in a few days the patient would be cured, no need to worry. So penicillin was given, but I was allergic to it. So I nearly died of penicillin, instead of pneumonia.

I felt so happy, so utterly peaceful lying there, floating a little. Soon I was in what seemed like a long tunnel. In the far distance was a light, a wonderful light that beckoned me to come. It was totally unlike any light that I had ever seen, impossible to describe. I wanted to get to it, because I knew I belonged to it as part of my whole being. I needed that Light.

Floating down the tunnel closer and closer, so happy, so at peace, my body was no longer a heavy burden, but full of joy at going towards the Light. No words can describe that Light: it was not of this world.

I was aware at the same time that my mother and sister were talking. I could hear my sister say, 'Is there no hope?' and my mother's reply, 'No, she is going now.' The Light told me to go back. I had to obey.

It was a supreme experience, literally out of this world. There need be no fear of death — it is a return to the Light from whence we came.

On one level, light could be described as the absence of darkness. On another, it could be described as the absence of ignorance. Light and darkness are dual aspects of the Great Mother, creation and destruction. Light and water are the source of life.

The Sun God and the Moon Goddess, the direct light of the Sun and the reflected light of the Moon, were the natural objects of ancient worship. People saw the Moon as the rhythm of the birth cycle: at New Moon each month the conjunction was the fertilization and the waxing Moon symbolised the swelling of the womb.

Light is a protection from fear. The primeval fear of the dark suffered by some children and also by some adults can be dispelled by blue light; a miniature blue light bulb on the bedroom floor gives peace. Blue light is the colour of the great deep as the feminine principle; it is the colour of the Great Mother and as such gives a feeling of being protected by love and gentleness.

I've often wondered if a blue light in a room where a baby is sleeping would prevent cot death. An old soul of many incarnations can enter this world in the tiny body of a new-born baby. During the current period of change, from the Age of Pisces to the Age of Aquarius, many old souls may be coming in to help with the transition in consciousness needed at this time. The healthy baby sleeping peacefully may dream of the World of Light from whence its soul came — the world where there was no necessity to breathe. It may be possible that the baby forgets to breathe, because it is dreaming of the Light. But if the room was bathed in blue light, the colour of the Great Mother, it would link the child to Earth. Satellite photographs show Earth as a beautiful blue planet, floating in space.

The healing power of coloured light is now recognised by some enlightened therapists. These 'colour' therapists can beam to the patients whatever colour is necessary to help them overcome their problem. This can be actual physical light, or Light on another level of awareness.

All but the physically blind can see light in many forms (sunlight, moonlight, artificial light), but those with the gift of sensitive awareness can see Light on another dimension altogether. This is the magnetic field that surrounds all people and all things; it can vary in width for many reasons. Seeing a spiritually evolved person talking to an audience, with the body at peace and wisdom flowing from their lips, the Light is strong and wide around the speaker who, through the Light, is acting as a channel for wisdom to flow through, without effort from the physical body.

The physical eyes see light; the eyes of the soul see Light. Some can see Light unexpectedly when sitting quietly in a dreamy state, with the eyes open but not really looking, possibly in a Church or some other peaceful place, when there appears to be Light around a person or object in the vicinity. But when they jerk back to reality and use their physical eyes, the Light is gone. They think they were dreaming; but it was no dream — it was reality on another dimension.

When the physical body is peaceful, the Light surrounds it. But when the body is restless and agitated, with the arms moving and gesticulating, the Light is broken up, dispersed, and knowledge cannot flow through; then there is only physical effort without inspiration.

To function on this planet Earth, the soul needs a physical body. Therefore it is essential to keep this body healthy, so that the soul can function at ease. We come from the World of Light to planet Earth, from spatial freedom to imprisonment in a human body. When They told me I was being sent to Earth for yet another incarnation, I told Them I did not want to go and begged Them not to send me. For years, I was bewildered by the restriction of the prison of a human body and so was frequently ill since I did not know how to cope with it. Eventually, I learned how to keep it healthy, though it was never easy. It is possible that many people have the same problem, the real cause of which goes unrecognised by doctors.

The magic of sunrise seems to be a connecting link between the two worlds — of Light and of Earth. To be at an ancient site, a stone circle or a mound, to watch the first pale light spreading from the east, gradually becoming pink and brighter, satisfies the soul's longing. It is easy to understand how natural was the cult of the Sun God. The small birds are waking and twittering in the hedges. Larger birds are flying overhead towards the west; having risen with the sun, they are now going before it.

Today, there is almost a return to sun worship, though this time on the purely physical level. People leave the cold countries and go for sunshine holidays, when they can expose their bodies to hours of blistering sunlight every day for two weeks.

The soft flickering of candlelight creates a magic gentleness for prayer and meditation, the contemplation of peace outside oneself, the drawing towards one of food for the soul and awareness of invisible friends around. Gentle light from small lamps (rather than a strong ceiling light) creates a cosy atmosphere in a room. But very harsh strip lighting seems to create tension for some people; there are others who find the rays from television or computer screens upset them. Those who have a sensitive awareness, a psychic awareness, appear to be susceptible to light on every level.

The light at the base of the ancient stones may be created by the friction of underground water which seems to flow at these sites, making a small electric current. A dowser once said to me, 'There is light at the base of these stones. I don't see it, but I know it is there.' One can be aware of light on other levels than the physical.

According to the dictionary, light is 'the natural agent that stimulates sight and makes things visible'. According to the Bible, 'God is Light and in Him is no darkness at all' (1 John 1:5). It all depends on how you look at it!

Time and Space

The time we now keep and the calendar we now use have gradually evolved over many centuries into a system that is at last universally accepted.

Astronomical measurement is the basis of all time-keeping. The year is related to the time it takes for the earth to travel around the sun. The day is related to the time it takes for the earth to rotate on its axis. These facts were the main reasons why ancient people the world over were so concerned with celestial happenings.

The ancient Egyptians, for example, needed to know when to expect the Nile to flood and irrigate the land. In ancient Ireland, too, in our cold climate we needed to know when to expect the shortest day and the longest day, so that we could know when to sow and harvest. Hence, the construction of Newgrange and other time-keeping sites.

Looking at the old traditional symbols, Time is the creator and the devourer; it is a destructive force, with Chronos or Saturn with his scythe representing the reaper. But Time is also the revealer of Truth. In the fairy tales of childhood, 'once upon a time' made all things seem possible.

To me, time is not a straight line. I feel it all around me — I can float forwards or backwards or sideways in time; I can see the past or the future or the present in another place.

Time out in space is not the same as time on planet Earth. One can muse on the possibility of ancient people being capable of space travel, as we read in the folktales of many countries. In our own Celtic mythology, you remember how Oisin went to Tir-na-nÓg with Niamh of the Golden Hair, where he lived for more than three hundred years, though it appeared to him that only three years had passed. Then he had a desire to visit his family and friends in Ireland. Niamh warned him three times not to get off the white horse, as she knew everything had changed — his family and friends were long gone. But Oisin accidentally fell from the horse; his youth faded rapidly and he became a withered old man.

When you travel out in space away from Earth, you go backwards in time. When you travel towards Earth, you go forwards in time. Because the light from the most distant galaxy observable through the most powerful telescope has taken about two billion years to reach us, the whole history of our planet is stored out in space, as if on a long strip of film, ready to be recalled by a person with the gift of travelling through time — and so through space.

When I was a child, I lived in Co Cork. In those days, there were three kinds of time: New Time, Old Time and God's Time. When our family were invited to visit another family's house, we first had to check which time they kept. New Time was Daylight Saving Time (or Summer Time, as it is now more usually known). Many country people would not change their clocks, because they considered it was bad for the animals to feed them an hour earlier or to milk the cows an hour before their usual time. So they kept Old Time. Their clocks were set at winter time all through the year. When they wanted to travel by bus or train, they had to remember that public transport ran by New Time in summer.

Then there was God's Time. This is true local time, as shown by the sundial; when the sun is at its highest point over each place, the local sundial indicates noon at that place. Before the 1880s, this was the time that people kept. But sundial time varies from place to place. As you move through longitude, you move through time: one degree of longitude is equal to four minutes of time. When a sundial at Greenwich indicates 12 noon, a sundial in Dublin would indicate 25 minutes earlier and a sundial in Galway would be 11 minutes earlier again, or 36 minutes earlier than Greenwich.

In the days when transport was by horse or by foot, this variety of time did not really matter; it took 'a long time' to get anywhere in any case. But when the railways started up in about 1850, there was quite a problem in deciding what time to get to the station for your train. However, this problem was solved by running the trains on the time at Dunsink Observatory. The guards on the trains leaving Dublin set their watches by Dunsink Time, then they gave this time to the station masters at each stop, who set their clocks to coincide. So we now had 'railway time' as well as local time. Some towns had two clocks — one showing railway time, the other local time. Intending passengers could now be sure of the correct time to be at the railway station, if they looked at the right clock!

In 1883, Dunsink Time was legally adopted as official government time for the whole country. If some people preferred to keep local time, they knew that all public affairs were run by Dunsink Time. This lasted until 1916, when from 21 May to 30 September we first kept Summer Time. Then, on 1 October 1916, we changed to Greenwich Mean Time and abolished Dunsink Time. This change was necessary due to the speeding up of transport; with the invention of the motor car and the greater speed of the trains, it simplified movement between Ireland and Britain by co-ordinating timetables.

Greenwich Mean Time is now used worldwide as Universal Time with a 24-hour day, from which the earth is divided into time zones. But there are only four dates in the year when the day is *actually* 24 hours: these are 16 April, 15 June, 2 September and 26 December. These dates can vary by one day. The difference is called the Equation of Time and can vary up to 16 minutes, since the clock can be slower or faster than the actual sun time. This difference is caused because the earth's path around the sun is not circular (it is an ellipse) and so the earth moves fastest when it is closest to the sun. For time-keeping, a fictitious mean sun is used which is assumed to travel at a constant rate along the celestial equator. It completes one circuit of this in the same length of time that the real sun takes to go around the ecliptic.

Though we adopted GMT, we did not always synchronise with Britain; when during the war years Britain kept double summer time, we did not. There is a government publication, *Standard Time and Summer Time*, which gives all the dates for changing the clocks since Daylight Saving first started. It is available from the Department of Justice or the Irish Astrological Association (193 Lower Rathmines Road, Dublin 6).

As for the date — well, that depended on the place until calendars were synchronised worldwide. In prehistoric times, it may have originated as an upright stick casting shadows of varying lengths at different seasons; these shadows may have been marked by incisions on the ground and these may have evolved into perpetual calendars in the form of stone circles and mounds.

Many early calendars were based on the lunar month. The Celts, for example, used a three-year lunar calendar. It was a simple method of incorporating the monthly lunar cycle with the feminine life rhythm; the four Great Festivals were held every three years, each festival separated by nine months.

The Irish ritual calendar began with the Samhain festival on 1st November. Nine months later came the summer festival of Lugnasadh on 1st August. A further nine months passed and Bealtaine was celebrated on 1st May. Precisely nine months later, Imbolc was held on 1st February. Nowadays, when we think of our festivals at all, we put them all into one year: Samhain on 1st November, Imbolc on 1st February, Bealtaine on 1st May and Lugnasadh on 1st August. This, of course, puts them in the wrong order, but we are more likely to remember them!

Many different calendars have been used throughout the ages. Each race seemed to have had its own system. To name a few, there were the early Roman, the Jewish, Greek, Muslim, Egyptian, Hindu and Chinese calendars; in the Americas, there were the Mexican Aztec, Peruvian Inca and Maya calendars. Some are still in use, but only for religious or ceremonial purposes.

The basic unit in any calendar is the day, which is measured from mid-night to mid-night. But this was not always so. Early civilizations used a dawn-to-dawn reckoning: the Babylonians and Greeks counted a day from sunrise to sunrise, while the Jews went from sunset to sunset.

Obviously, it is quite impossible to discuss every civilization's calendar. It is a vast subject, so let us see how our present calendar evolved. In 46 BC, Julius Caesar, with the help of an astronomer from Egypt named Sosigenes, laid down the Julian calendar, using the sun as the guide. This solar calendar was a great improvement, but not totally accurate; it amounted to an error of one day in 128 years. So, by 1545 the Spring Equinox had moved ten days from its proper date. When the Council of Trent met that year, it asked Pope Paul III to take action to correct the matter. However, neither Paul nor his immediate successors were able to work out a satisfactory solution.

By the time Pope Gregory XIII was elected in 1572, he found various ideas for a new calendar awaiting him. He put two astronomers, Christopher Clavius and Luigi Lilio, to work and in 1582 the Gregorian calendar was devised. Ten days had been dropped in order to correct the date and bring the Spring Equinox back to 21st March. To bring the year closer to the true tropical year, a value of 365.2422 days was accepted. A century year was not always a Leap Year; it had to be exactly divisible by 400 to be so.

This Gregorian calendar is the one still in use today, although it has a slight error of less than half a minute, which would amount to one day in 3300 years. But Gregory's calendar was not accepted immediately by all countries. Only France, Italy, Luxembourg, Portugal and Spain adopted it in 1582. Other countries followed slowly with, for example, Sweden making the change in 1753, Japan in 1873, Egypt in 1875, Russia in 1918 and Greece as late as 1923.

In Britain and Ireland, and in the British dominions, the change to the Gregorian calendar was made in 1752, when the difference between the calendars had mounted to eleven days — the day after 2nd September 1752 became 14th September, to the alarm of all!

Now that we have achieved worldwide agreement on time and on calendars, perhaps an era will come when we can achieve worldwide agreement on all things: on peace instead of war, on love instead of hate, on true spirituality instead of religious bickering, on enlightenment instead of ignorance.

Metaphysical Values

9

The metaphysical values need to be appreciated in a general sense. Science, religion, philosophy and art are the spokes of our great wheel of civilization. The energy created by these ideas should bring humanity into a realisation of itself and its purpose in this beautiful cosmic reality. We need to unblock our minds so that we can grow naturally into new ideas and be creative in these areas. They are all linked, so progress can be made from 'flat-earth' thinking to esoteric ideas. With the pure intellect of research, science can mechanically use energies which the artist can then demonstrate in poetry and painting, which religion can exhibit in faith, which the philosopher can link to within his vision.

Science uses the power of observation and experiment to repeat a phenomenon; this describes a law that defines an affinity to an energy. Life and consciousness and light are all energies; science, in investigating life, is a form of self-contemplation. As each energy is more deeply understood, humanity is in the position of choosing between atomic bombs and a drug-ridden society, or developing the metaphysical values of a higher science that links in to the beauty of an appreciation of life. Science opens up the minute world, the microcosm, to find the reflection of the macrocosm, and gives an appreciation of an orderliness in creation where life is controlled by invisible forces within which there is a potential of power and energy that is ceaseless, eternal, perpetual.

But the crisis is the primitive man motivating the technical man and thus we see the industries of war and technical slavery. Esoterically, we appreciate the concept of the spiritual side which can override the material side, and so there is a need for bi-dimensional co-operation. Spiritual scientists and earth scientists already do this. With the present expansions of human consciousness, many great inventions are on the fringe of discovery and await the work of metaphysical value, before mankind can be entrusted with the knowledge.

True spiritual science gives a reverence for all life and a respect for all the forces of nature. It creates a bridge between science and spiritual ideas. Primitive people link into natural science, but when people became materialistic and scientific they lost the Ancient Wisdom and believed instead that they were omnipotent.

Religion links to the invisible, which can be sensed, and the overall purpose can be brought into an organised form, a code of behaviour both for health and social security. An initiate can hold a structure, but religion can constrict through too literal an interpretation. Crystallisation needs to be broken and re-directed; religion should be natural law which indicates natural instincts. Different religions show the way to God through different aspects of the consciousness, though there is a common basis; adding knowledge to faith gets rid of medieval nonsense.

So much of the mystical side of religion has been suppressed. The Ancient Wisdom, of man's attunement to the universal forces, is now frowned upon and disowned by the churches. The true and ancient spiritual science of astrology is condemned by clergy and debased in the press. Humanity's natural attunement to the heavens through the ancient stones, the circles, the lone megaliths, the geodetic forces, are all written off by the organised religions as heathen mumbo-jumbo.

True mysticism, true knowledge, is, however, being poured into people's awareness from the cosmos and no ignorant denunciations can stop its return. Those of us who are aware of the Light are attuning ourselves to these invisible forces and learning to work with them. The cleaning of the atmosphere, the meditative concentration, the total awareness and dedication to the Work are reminiscent of the scientist working on the material plane in his laboratory. Then, a state of happiness comes in to our lives as we become aware of something greater and beyond ourselves that we can tune into and use for the universal good; no longer do we have to cope with the physical world on our own. The most practical person is the true mystic who will bring the higher knowledge down to the physical plane and use it in a pragmatic way.

There are many paths all leading to the same goal. Each person needs to evolve in their own way: the path for one may not suit the footsteps of another, so that one becomes broad-minded and understanding of the problems encountered. We should each look over our shoulder at those struggling after us and offer our hand and heart to bring them up the next step — 'Do not walk in front of me, I might not be able to follow; do not walk behind me, I might not be able to lead; just walk beside me and be my friend.'

Philosophy is more universal than religion. There is seeded into humanity a knowledge that gives vision beyond religion — cosmic knowledge. There is a universal concept so that problems of the time can find an on-going relationship; a philosophy that links to the Ageless Wisdom is ever alive.

We need the philosopher-scientist, the philosopher-religionist. Humanity is reaching up. These are exciting times — we live on the edge of discovery of all that exists. Meditation opens the consciousness to the wider concept; contemplation allows the natural inflow of the universal knowledge. But we can reach a point where we have studied enough and then it is time to get out and be involved in life in a constructive way. We should give of our originality, allow at least a little of what we have learnt to rub off on other people.

The philosopher can stand apart, detached, observing, seeing how both science and religion can serve humanity when they get beyond their narrow-minded confines. The philosopher can, on the wings of his imagination, create a whole new world of beauty where people are served by things, rather than enslaved by them. It is anathema to philosophical concepts to see people enslaved to machines, standing bored in production lines day after day doing the same monotonous task that gives no aesthetic satisfaction. The machine age took from people the creative urge to produce in tangible form with their own hands a complete article that satisfied both mind and soul.

Today we see more and more people are abandoning the 'rat race' and turning to creative pursuits — weaving, painting, carpentry, crafts that feed their hungry souls. Financially, they may not be so well off, but they are happy and contented. Some babies are being born naturally at home in the family atmosphere rather than in hospitals.

The philosopher is needed in this world to create the dreams that create a future, to draw humanity's consciousness towards beauty in all things — 'with all its sham, drudgery and broken dreams it is still a beautiful world.' The astronauts who have looked on our planet from far out in space have seen a very wonderful blue orb floating through time.

Art is re-creation. There is art in everything. The concept of art links to the moment of creation; within the theme of the living moment it is involved with a sense of time. Nature is the greatest artist of all — the seasonal variations, the natural challenges, respond to the fullest measure in the outward expression of the myriad of divine blueprints within all nature's forms. But humanity works within the primal energy's re-creation when, through the emotions, colour and shape are used to decorate and create its personal environs. The recognition of a rhythm within creation can be expressed in body movement and sound that link to the wind and the sea and the natural elements. Man imitates nature through his art, where the creative potential is stimulated, inspired by a spiritual vision; this brings a sense of harmony and beauty and symmetry that translates and refines the primal energies into areas of service to the future.

As a measurement, the level of art within a culture indicates the degree of attunement or otherwise; in therapy all art forms through their rhythmic action will find a response within the senses that is both cleansing and regenerative. Socially, we realise the value of the environment and the influence of art in an atmosphere. Within religion, art has found inspiration; in science, art demonstrates another application of precision; in philosophy, art becomes the poetry and song that speaks directly to the soul. The artistic and creative side is essential. We need beauty around us, we need to create with our minds and our hands to be whole people. An ugly, materialistic, non-creative life is soul-destroying; it promotes tensions from within. Suffering humanity has created most of its own dis-eases because it is out of tune with the harmony of nature, unaware of the natural will-to-good that is waiting to be tapped; in a finer vibration, many states of disease and disharmony fall away, so that one is in tune with all life.

Art is the beautiful quality that exists in all things. The artist is creating beauty just as much in prayer, in vision, in science, as in a beautiful painting or sculpture. Within ourselves are all the sounds and rhythms and colours of nature; as we link in and produce these ourselves, we become in touch with the universal forces. Then science will not totally control the factories, because true religion and philosophy will flourish and expand humanity's understanding of the necessity for beauty in all things. In the casting-off of our 'protective concealments', truth and beauty can stand revealed and healing can take place.

Protective Concealments

It is not always safe to expose ourselves. It is often dangerous to show our hand too soon. So to protect themselves all life forms blend into the environment, creating a natural camouflage. The herd gives them safety; if one strays or dares to be different, it can be destroyed by others. Chameleons change their colour to blend into the background, also to establish an identity.

Mankind does the same for survival: there is the tribal sense, the different languages, the skin colours, the social classes, the group sense. In medieval times, there was protection in the trade you were born into. An organisation is a way of surviving — the clergy wear different clothes, the various religions give their followers a sense of security. The drop-outs go around in their groups, in their uniforms of spiked hair and studded plastic jackets. We get the herds of people dressed in their 'robes of office' — business men in bowler hats and striped suits, politicians recognisable in their group behaviour.

But individuals need to emerge from the group and establish their own identity. The consciousness forms an association for each incarnation. It identifies itself with certain work; all identities exist in each of us, we need all experiences. The incarnating ego takes different roles associated with the elements fire/earth/air/water, so giving the ego different elemental energies.

An historical background is essential to the consciousness — to be in it, but not of it, to develop detachment so that one can assess a situation. The consciousness draws to itself many cloaks and disguises as it descends and enters the different vibrational levels of experience. On the earth it must work in with the nature happenings of protective resemblance as it identifies with its work area within the primal energies. Natural protection exists through the blending of colour and design, that the life forms may evolve within an harmonious interdependence. The instinct, the group mind, the characteristics of a species, all identify with common resemblance.

The social evolution of mankind has historically worked through a system of castes and structured roles in society. At this time, we see the group identity in uniforms that represent basic security areas in man's thinking. These include the army, organised religion, certain professions; this is a professional camouflage. In this sense there is a visible contribution, but in the artificial sense we see the veneer.

Over the state of conflict and dishonesty that exists in the world today, there is a strange veneer of everybody wanting peace and goodwill. The veneer is a superficial covering that says, 'to maintain peace we must develop armaments and drugs and charities.' But the reality is extortion and deception. So many people have a veneer, a pretence, pretending to be what they are not: wishing to be considered holy, giving lip service, but inwardly full of evil thoughts.

Education can also give a veneer: the self-made millionaire giving his son the benefit of the type of education that was totally out of reach when he was young. People create a situation that suits their own veneer. But the true consciousness can sometimes emerge if we appeal to the better side of a person's nature. There are times when a veneer is put on to conceal an inadequacy (an introverted person being aggressive, for example), or to deceive or to compensate; but beyond a certain point it lowers the tone of life. We see the false front or dishonest exterior that is common at every level and that associates to deception, that is not so much protective as cunning.

A therapist needs to have an awareness of social and professional veneers, since they conceal the area through which many lives are drawn into unnatural response and disharmony. The veneer is a precursor of energy imbalances. As this becomes more deep-seated, it motivates and colours basic attitudes.

These veneers really conceal attitudes that go very deep, that are historical. And what is history is Karma. We see even in the present age disagreements and injustices that are linked to disharmonies of centuries ago; they taint the environment and need to be changed. The New Age ideas bring one up against traditional attitudes in countries where old attitudes and religious dogmatism conflict with the new ideas of people who have visited other countries, or who innately feel the Aquarian influences. If the attitude is changed, then the problem disappears; it is necessary to get away from prejudice, away from fixations, to escape into the clear air, the open mind. The Quakers changed people's attitude to mental hospitals and prisons by going into these places and seeing for themselves what they were really like; they brought into the open what had been despised and turned people's minds to a more compassionate attitude.

Rather than give a command to change, it is better to plant a thought in people's minds that will hopefully take root and eventually blossom as a changed attitude. There is no sense in sitting in judgment on dead and past situations, it is a form of self-punishment. Let the past go, forgive both oneself and others.

The basic attitudes to develop include attitudes towards illness, tolerance, security, survival; and so lessen the flexibility of thought and response. We say there are no problems, only attitudes of mind. The attitude of people towards their own condition is the key to their ability to respond, which we call their responsibility.

Historical veneers and attitudes lead to deep fear and become concealed in the subconscious where their origin is forgotten; they can become part of the identity that can corrupt a lifetime and negatively motivate the response of the consciousness to growth opportunities. Here the therapist works within the philosophy field offering comparative ideas, so that the deep-seated fixations may be re-associated into something constructive and worthwhile.

Concealment is in the deep subconscious and can become a motivating force that colours and ruins our lives. A concealment area, where there are deep-seated fears, phobias and fixations, needs to be gone into deeply in therapeutic work. An association can free it, but therapy must be done at the level that is available, where a person is asking for help; our mind should be able to tune into and reflect the situation. An incarnation can be wasted unless the person is willing to change and forget historical associations.

In the body there are also many associations we hold in balance, such as the thyroid which can cause depression or the opposite. In a psychic nature, the gland balance can be critical. People need to learn to work with nature, not against it. Natural foods and remedies supply the right balance, as also do breathing and rhythmic movements. We do not have to conflict with medicine, rather make suggestions to a person about natural healing; before Lister was ever heard of, healing herbs were known and used.

Self-discipline involves the right use of the situation; true freedom is when the free will is not used by the ego, but comes from the super-conscious. Physical healing alone is not enough, the philosophy should come into it: change the tensions and it eases the body. The consciousness needs tough energy fields. It is necessary to develop an attitude that gives a choice; a therapist can give support, but the person must work through it.

With negative concealment, there is the need to release the past and feed in a new attitude toward all life forms, to approach every aspect freely within the direct identity of the consciousness associated with the natural protections. To bring a person from the past to the future needs each therapist and counsellor to be an example within their own situation and, at the same time, to be purely and simply themselves. Esoterically exposure to the truth may be uncomfortable, but it is the finest experience for natural growth. Then there are no secrets and all will in time be released into its potential.

Magnetic Field

For many years I used to think that the light I saw around people was their soul shining out around their body. Some people's souls were big and bright, others were so close to the body that they were scarcely visible. Most people were in between the two. I used to wonder why the soul did not fit the body properly, instead of sticking out all around it. Then I thought that perhaps it was protecting the body, like an armour of light.

I was always aware of people's personal light. I was surprised that so few people saw it and hurt when they thought I was talking nonsense. I learned to keep my knowledge to myself, unless I was with kindred spirits. But there were not very many of them around.

Here I would like to put in a plea for children with spiritual gifts: a child born with the gift of seeing and hearing on a higher level of consciousness can be totally warped in a materialistic family. The child is rebuked for telling lies and making up stories, so that he or she will eventually become shy and introverted, because of being made to feel 'different'.

When I began to meet people on my own 'wavelength', I realised that what I was seeing was the magnetic field. This is around everything, not just people. It may be that it is through the magnetic field that dowsers get their information. When a dowser concentrates on the object that is being sought, the magnetic field of the dowser could be attracting the magnetic field of the object.

As each field reaches out and connects with the other field, the dowser is aware of the reaction through the pendulum or rods. So the magnetic field is light on another dimension.

We all know that the earth has a magnetic field; when we use a compass it points to magnetic north. Magnetism attracts and also repulses. It is what keeps the planets in their orbits around the sun; by attracting and repulsing each other they keep a perfect balance and do not collide.

When I am using my pendulum, I see a bright light shining around it. But if I concentrate on the work for too long, the light disappears and the pendulum will not move. I think this is a natural safety mechanism to save one from 'blowing a fuse'.

In ancient days I believe that people had a great knowledge of the power of light and that this knowledge was lost when the world became materialistic. Some of this knowledge seems to be returning as we move into the New Age. It is possible that everything above and below and around us is linked to us and through us by the magnetic field — this light that surrounds everything.

There need be no clash between ancient technology and today's 'high tech'. The dowser can find the flow of energies in the ancient natural way. But for people without this gift, modern technology has invented the detector, which will find anything from a gas pipe to a buried chalice. Again, an astrology chart involves calculations that can be quite tedious, but by using a computer, they can be done in seconds. The ancient computers are made of stone and have calculated the position of celestial bodies for thousands of years; Newgrange and other megalithic sites are the high technology of their age. By using dowsing or psychometry, one can feel the energies in these sites. But now, some people use detectors on the stones to find a reaction.

What we are seeing nowadays is the great explosion of knowledge in this century in the field of high technology. We also see the great explosion of interest in the Ancient Knowledge. By keeping an open mind on both levels, they will come together and one day modern technology will prove the truth and accuracy of the knowledge that spiritually gifted people possess in their own natural way.

Reincarnation

As we get more and more into esoteric ideas, we realise that we knew all this before, in the past of long ago. The cloud of ignorance is being removed, so that the innate universal knowledge is once more coming through. The Ancient Wisdom is all around us for those whose eyes are open to see and whose ears are open to hear. The doors of the Great University of Space open to those who knock, to those who thirst for Truth.

We find a bridge has been created which takes us from the many questions to which life cannot supply an answer to a way of seeing ourselves and all people as bi-dimensional structures, both physical and spiritual. We can study this structure from primitive survival instincts and come to know of the energy forms through which this Earth body has its life. Through this life the bi-dimensional body links through all nature and all life forms, right back to the source.

We learn how to bring in a relationship and treat the person in a practical way through the gravity and magnetic fields that join us to the Earth and to the stars. We come to realise that there is a psychic or astral body, with its chakras that function through the physical body as the main organs and nerves and glands. We become aware that illness and disease happen when these bodies are out of balance. We can learn a form of therapy where we can re-align the magnetic and gravity fields, so bringing the physical body into balance with the non-physical body.

We learn to work within the atmosphere of a person, to be more the counsellor who can become aware of a person's problems and so make that person aware of their problems in such a way that their consciousness can be re-directed. The mind can make the body ill, so that by changing one's thought forms, the body is encouraged to heal itself. Mother Nature will respond if given the opportunity; we can make suggestions, so encouraging the person to be their own therapist, to heal themselves.

We become ever more aware of new valuations; spiritual awareness and intellectual appreciation give a sensitivity that reaches out into the wider society. The materialistic outlook of the world can physically affect in an adverse way the sensitive people who need to function on a higher level of awareness. Hopefully, they learn to be in it but not of it, to release their tensions, to be able to relate on all levels, through functioning inwardly on their own awareness. They 'know' as well as understand.

Eventually, the practical Mystic will function where the practical state of outer awareness is joined with the mystical state of inner awareness, becoming very aware of the reality of the inner world, as it can function in a viable way through the outer world. By knowing the value of mystical experience and of the relativity of time, one can move forward or backward or sideways through time; there can be parallel experiences where the physical body is in one place, while the person has been seen elsewhere.

We absorb knowledge all the time from the atmosphere. Quite often a disaster can become a stepping stone to more awareness; maybe we have become stuck in a rut and we need a disaster to jerk us out of it and move forward. But we should not expect privileges from the spiritual level. We gradually develop a sense of timing where we can work on impulse. There are times when the energy is there, so we learn to feel it and work with the tide of energy; if we try to work against it we become exhausted. Even Jesus could not do this in Nazareth because of their unbelief; at other times he knew 'the power of the Lord was present for healing'.

When we look more closely at the Aura, we realise that this energy pattern flows and reflects into life; when there is a break or distortion in any of the colour fields of the Aura it shows an illness, or potential illness, within that area. When people develop their ability to see or feel the Aura, then medicine will become preventative rather than, as is usual now, wait until illness strikes and then go looking for a cure. The human body usually survives through the instincts.

By examining the Wheel of Life, we become aware of the different levels of consciousness. In the Deep Karmic level are buried memories of previous incarnations. It is from here that over-shadowing takes place; the deep wisdom of our over-self gathered from all previous incarnations takes over the life, so then we can work more deeply into these other areas.

An awakening takes place as the deep subconscious begins to manifest. We develop a sense of affinity with all life and become free of prejudice, free of the environmental situation. We draw in the qualities and spiritual awareness that is necessary to cope with the situation. The Karmic mind flows in in different ways and we become more aware of different aspects of ourselves, both the good and the bad. We know that only a fragment of our consciousness incarnates.

All events in our life are for our training, whether pleasant or unpleasant, hurtful or loving. From every experience something can be learnt and used when a similar situation turns up again, whether in our own or another person's life; the lesson from the previous experience can be a pattern to cope with it this time. Through the spiral of evolvement, it can come through at a higher level and be used with spiritual intelligence. We need humility, so that we work from our inner guide in service to the evolutionary principle as we rise through the levels of the spiral of life, rather than stick at the same old place.

In working for others we need to use detached compassion, detached involvement, not to get so emotionally entangled in their problems that we cannot work intelligently. Be there until they can stand on their own feet, point them in the right direction, then allow them to live their own lives.

With the new recognition that everything is spiritual, that our previous incarnations are living in us now, we can accept the joy of life as it is now. We see that though the body may age, we become spiritually youthful; we alter ideas and attitudes that we have got hooked on and accept life as a natural sequence of events. The patterns of consciousness weaving into Earth life overshadow and reflect the interaction within the third dimensional fields; this links to the individual purpose and joins with the destiny and adjusts in its reflection, according to the way the life is lived.

The teachings of reincarnation, suppressed for many centuries, are now being reintroduced where there is a back log of suppressed Karmic history; to enable each Earth life to work through many incarnations can then be compressed into one. As the realisation of an attunement to this grows, there is gradually the drawing closer of the over-soul where an over-shadowing of the human aura by the reincarnation aura can occur. Awareness is deepened, capacities grow and the equality of each life also grows in every area. It brings a sense of detachment and acceptance and humility, that each in their own field gradually becomes a mini-teacher, mini-master, mini-messiah.

So we find a new recognition to the essential consciousness as a practical involvement of our inter-dimensional structures, within the confines of time and space. Its importance directly relates to the cleansing and preparation for the New Age in mankind's consciousness and it provides an anchor that will protect and guide us during the period ahead.

Meditation

I meditate, I go in, I meet the Self, I am that I am. I am in God. God is in me. I am God. God is me. We are one.

I meditate on a rose, I enter the rose. The rose enters me. I am that rose. We are one.

I meditate on a tree. I enter the tree. The tree enters me. We are one.

I meditate on a human soul, weary, sad and ill. I enter that soul. It enters me. We are one. The troubles are shared, two now carry the load, so it is lighter, much lighter.

Beyond the five senses all is one. God in everything. Everything in God. All is Light. All is well.

The ever-ascending spiral from matter to space consciousness evolving upwards and outwards. Accepting that which is; moving then to higher things.

I think, the thought gathers force, a pattern forms. The hands obey. Creation moves a pace. An artifact is born.

In and out we move, not in one world, but many, visible and invisible. Some we may touch and feel, others we perceive but cannot touch. We know. We see. Past, present, future are all around for us to see.

Time is, yet time is not. Sun, Moon, Planets moving in their cycles. The whole cosmos is reflected in each human body. Our birth moment sets our time in tune with space.

Our soul is a spark from the fire of God; pure cosmic fire to burn the dross, to purify the incarnation. The planet holds the body, as the soul, the spark, yearns to return from whence it came.

All is motion. The eternal dance of Shiva on the earth and quantum physics both agree — there is no solid matter. We live and move and have our being through many incarnations; learning, evolving, accepting the challenge, balancing the opposites.

It's love that makes the world go round, that binds all things, that heals all ills, that reveres all life, that will live and let live.

If we 'become as little children' we can accept the wonder of life, bypass the intellect and see God in everything, visible and invisible.

We know, but know not how we know. We understand, but cannot explain to others, until they also 'know'.

The New Age dawn is breaking. The birth pangs of Aquarius are traumatic; the travail must be gone through. It is hard work for those who are giving birth. But when we see the Light appear in the eyes of others, we rejoice. 'Praise God from whom all blessings flow'.

Sunrise

We went to Tara for the summer solstice sunrise on a beautiful clear morning. The sun rose as predicted, at 4.57 am. My thoughts that rose with it were spoken aloud and written down by Anne.

The earth is dipping down into the Sun. The Soul of Ireland is buried in this place. It is very holy. The soul has to come out of hiding. Tara will come into its own when the time is here.

I feel that it is necessary to find the right people and get them to understand what has to be done. I think this place had to have a quiet time. But the time is coming near when it has to be used again.

I think that it is almost more important than Newgrange. Tara has to do with the fullness of life, and Newgrange the birth. Almost as if it has generated Newgrange.

There is a feeling as if there are crowds of people and they are waiting for someone to wake them up. There are an awful lot of people here.

There is a great sheet of darkness and there are streaks of lightning breaking the darkness. This lightning seems to be splitting. The darkness is ignorance, it is not real darkness. It is as if it is lifting and they are holding up their hands, almost as if they were pushing it away. The light is a sort of white light coming down. It is almost as if the people were dancing.

There is a great feeling of holiness. Somebody said it has to come again. Something to do with yellow again. I don't know what that is.

The whole ground is alive; and yet it is asleep and needs to be brought awake . . .

Alpha and Omega

What is an ending, but a chance to make a new beginning.
Or what is a beginning, but a chance to end that which is completed.
What is the end of the Old Year, but the beginning of the New Year;
Or the end of Winter, but the beginning of Spring.
What are beginnings and endings, but progressions in life,
The rungs on the ladder toward expansion of experience.
Without movement and change we stagnate and decay.
Each experience in life can be accepted and used for development;
Or rejected and resented, as unjust punishment from an unjust God.

The beginning of our life in this world is the temporary end of our life in the Spiritual.
But the ending of life here is the beginning of the return to whence we came.
We choose our incarnations to gain experience, to evolve, to absolve Karma.
The pure spirit enters the soul for physical birth, or spiritual death;
But the soul leaves the physical body for spiritual birth, or bodily death.
The caterpillar dies, so the butterfly can rise on wings of joy,
Freed from the body that kept it tied to earth.

There is no need for fear. I know. I have been there. But I came back.
There was that Light, that glorious indescribable Light;
The Light of pure joy, pure love and utter peace
That beckoned me on, that drew me towards my true home,
Floating freely, as the butterfly free of the mortal body.
And then the voices of those I was leaving:
'Is there no hope?' 'No, she is going.'
And the Light said, 'Not yet. Go back. There is work for you to do.'

GOD IS LIGHT

About the Author

SHEILA LINDSAY was born in Co. Cork. She is a founder member and past president of the Irish Astrological Association and a founder member of Waymark, a branch of the College of Psychotherapeutics. She is also a member of the Irish Society of Diviners. She teaches astrology and dowsing, and frequently lectures on these and other subjects.

Photographic credits: (between pages 48-49) Photographs 1-4, 6-8, Office of Public Works, Ireland; Photograph 5, Mary Dunphy; Photograph 9, James Bambury; Photograph 10, Trinity College Dublin.